Desert Duel

When rancher Juan Valdes was found murdered, having been killed by a strange bullet, it lit a trail that burned like gunpowder to an explosion of such violence that the badlands were set aflame. The thunder of guns echoed in the rocky ravines and the sands were stained red.

From the shadows, treachery, deceit and cynically planned murder were dragged into the full glare of the desert sun and stretched across the path of the young deputy, Cal Rogers and his girl.

It was savage going as they struggled to find an answer to a mystery, which the power of the Law could not solve. Could they succeed?

ONE

The big man lay sprawling in the dirt of the rough track which passed within quarter of a mile of his own front door. He was face downwards and the back of his head had been blown in at close range so that his black, greying hair was singed with exploded gunpowder. It was a mess of blood and bone. His dark jacket was twisted around as if he had half-turned as he fell and it had slipped partly off one shoulder, exposing a hint of white shirt and blue cravat, both now spattered in dried blood. What could be seen of his face was deeply tanned, swarthy behind his short neat beard. The rest of his clothing looked smart and clean, considering where they had been lying, and his knee-high boots seemed newly polished.

Valdes had been a proud man, who wished,

when his hands were not at the plough or pulling a rope or dragging at a saw, to dress in his best clothes and look like a gentleman – a *señor* – as his father and grandfather had been, long years ago, in more prosperous times for his family, when all the wide country around had been Mexican.

Now the Texan sun burned into his back and the flies crawled over his wound, but all pride had gone from him and it did not matter any more how he might look to the small group of men who stood nearby, hats off in a gesture of respect for the dead, eyes curious, surprised, pitying, minds jumping in speculation.

'Took it full and close up, sure enough,' grunted Abe Hunter. 'Right in the back of the skull. . . .' He shook his balding head ruefully, expressing his disgust. 'Dirty piece of shootin'. Some yeller-belly, sure as hell!'

'You said it.' Mike Heston sounded bitter. He had always had a liking for Juan Valdes, respecting the man for his hard work and his determination over years of struggle to make a living for himself and his family from this wasted, wind-blown soil. He pursed his thin lips and looked down a long, freckled nose at the body. As sheriff, it fell to him now to find the murderer and bring him to justice. It was hard

6

to know just where to begin. There did not seem to be any reason for this crime. Valdes, for all his fine appearance, would have been carrying little or no money, for this, Heston knew, was the farmer's Sunday suit, from which he had not had time to change before death overtook him.

'Don't look like robbery,' grunted Deputy Ryan, seeming to echo his thoughts. 'Mr Valdes must have jest been on his way back from church.' He glanced at Heston, puzzled. 'Guess he must have lain out all night.'

It seemed queer, only a little way from home. The sheriff turned from looking at the body and peered at the rising slope of rough dry grass that blocked out his view of the farmstead. There came into his mind a vision of the Valdes family sleeping through the night while the head of the household lay dead a short distance away. Nobody at the place could have seen it happen, of course, but, jeeze, what were they thinking all night, knowing that he had not returned?

'Say, Pinky.' He was looking now at the little farm-help who had brought him the news only a couple of hours before. 'You say that Mrs Valdes was here – that she saw him?'

'Sure,' Pinky squinted out of his little eyes

and shook the tangle of straw-coloured hair which threatened to obscure his vision. 'She stood up on the bank thereabouts, then she waves me over. Told me to git into town and fetch you pronto. She was all-over cryin' – tearin' at her dress and cryin'.'

'Did she come down here to look at him? Did she touch anything?'

'Nope. She said that she could tell he was dead. Anybody could, o' course, by the look of him! I think she just went back to the house while I got my horse and rode like hell into Baxters.'

That bit was right anyhow. Pinky had arrived on a lather-covered horse at the sheriff's office in Baxterville when Heston was still pulling the blinds. He had needed a borrowed mount to ride the twelve miles back, in the company of Heston and Deputies Ryan and Hunter and young Cal Rogers, who had added himself to the party, not because he was a lawman, but because he had a kind of special interest in the Valdes place for his own personal reasons.

Young Cal wasn't looking too good. He was pale and strained and there were beads of sweat glistening under his fair hair. He wasn't used to seeing corpses – not like Heston and his henchmen, who had seen plenty in their time.

And, of course, this was Juan Valdes, and that meant something special to the youngster, as it did to a lesser extent to them all.

'I'll go and speak to Mrs Valdes,' announced Heston suddenly, turning to take his horse from Hunter. 'Maybe she can tell me somethin' more. You two have a good look around. See if there are any tracks or signs.'

The latter instruction was unnecessary, as he well knew. His deputies had plenty of experience and needed no telling. It was just that he wanted to speak to Mrs Valdes by himself.

'All right if I come too, Sheriff?'

The request from Cal interrupted his gathering train of thought and he glanced round in sharp irritation, but the youngster seemed full of earnest appeal and Heston at once relented. Cal would be wanting to see Maria. He must be worried about her, about how she must be taking this terrible shock. They weren't exactly sweethearts, these two, but there seemed to be something of an understanding, and they had been seen a couple of times, riding around in a buggy, with Cal at the reins, Maria beside him, while Mrs Valdes played chaperon in the back seat.

'Well, sure, but let me do the talking.'

They rode slowly and respectfully towards

9

the house, hats still held at their saddle bows. The building was a mixture of good stone and timber, made with much hard work and the best materials available. Only the outhouses were adobe. The nearby fields were given over to vegetables, drying out too quickly in the sun, in spite of the daily efforts of two Hispanics and a Negro to keep the plots well watered from the deep-bored well. There was nothing particularly Mexican about the appearance of the place, not until you saw the inside with its shabby curtains and carpets and well-preserved oaken furniture, which had come down to Valdes from his own family and been treasured by him ever since.

No one appeared at the doorway until Heston called out in a hesitant and respectful tone and then Mrs Valdes came out of the shadows like a ghost, her head half-covered by a dark veil. It was as if she was already in mourning. She did not look at them but stood in silence as if expecting some news of an even worse nature than had already come to her. She looked crushed and beaten. Even so, they felt a little surprised that she failed to invite them into the house.

'Mrs Valdes, I cain't tell you how sorry I am about your husband,' stammered Heston. He was not normally a nervous man but he found this situation unnerving. 'I'm sorry to trouble you but I need you to tell me all you know about what Juan was doing just before this happened. Did you see anybody else around? Did you hear anythin'? When did you last see him, exactly?'

'He went to church. We all went to church, as usual.' Her voice was low and hesitant. It held no trace of accent. She had no Mexican in her. She was North Texan but had adopted her husband's ways in all respects. 'When we got home he went out for an evening ride around the farm. That was the last I saw of him.'

'But when he didn't come back Mrs Valdes . . . ?'

'I thought maybe he had gone into town. Perhaps on some business or something.'

'On the Sabbath?' Heston sounded bluntly suspicious but then changed his tone swiftly back to one of sympathy and concern. 'Would he have been doin' anything like that on a Sunday?'

'Well, you know how it is . . .'

Her voice trailed off in indecision. Heston did not know how it was that she had thought that Juan could have ridden into Baxterville on a Sunday evening without telling her why. Some men might do something like that – the ones

11

who frequented the saloon with its lady enter-
tainers – but never on the Sabbath, and surely
not Juan Valdes!

'Yeah, but, Mrs Valdes, he didn't come back
all night. Pinky says you only found him this
mornin'. Did you not look around – send out
some of the men? And did you not know that his
horse is still in the stable? Pinky says he saw it
early this mornin', fresh as you like!'

'I don't know! I only thought he had gone to
Baxters! He doesn't tell me much of what's goin'
on. I really can't take all this talk, all this mad
noise and questioning! Juan's . . . dead. Oh,
God, he's dead . . . really dead. Oh, Jesus.'

She began to sink to her knees. Heston and
Cal leaped forward to catch her but then
stopped as she steadied herself against the wall
of the porch. At that moment, her daughter,
Maria, came from inside and gripped her
mother by the arm and around the waist.

'Please, Mr Heston, not now. My mother is too
shocked by this. It's just as she says, anyway.
She doesn't know what happened. I must try to
calm her.'

They vanished into the interior of the house.
For a moment the door swung open wide and
Cal saw Sebastian sitting there at the breakfast
table. The lad was stuffing food into his moon-

face but looked up grinning, the dull stupidity of his eyes hardly changing. Sebastian Valdes was sixteen years old but with the mental age of a very young child. Another burden for the family and one which had sometimes come near to breaking his father.

Cal turned away with the sheriff, feeling a little hurt that Maria had not spoken to him or appeared to have noticed him, although he could understand the reason for it. Within a few minutes they were back at the scene of death where the two deputies had turned the body over. The forehead and eyes were a mass of congealed blood, the bullet having blasted its way out through the right temple.

'Went in pretty low,' commented Hunter, seeing them staring, 'and came out high.' He was standing at the other side of the trail, holding Ryan's horse while Ryan was in the saddle, reaching up to dig into the bark of a tree with his Bowie knife. 'Looks like it went into this here pine.' He jerked up with his head. 'Ken was lookin' around and sees the bark all chipped out.'

Ken Ryan grunted confirmation. The white wood was flaking out under the scurry of his blade. He was going in pretty deep. Then the point touched metal and he grinned suddenly in

13

satisfaction. 'This is it! Have it out in no time now.'

'Could help if we kin find out the calibre,' explained Hunter, nodding at Cal, who nodded back in agreement.

'Looks like a thirty-eight near enough,' put in Heston. 'Hundreds of them around. Ain't likely to help much. Still, won't do no harm to have the bullet.'

'Here it comes,' said Ryan, then his voice turned to a yelp of surprise. 'Jeeze, what's this?'

He rubbed the bullet on his sleeve and then held it up to the light. It was silver in colour and perfectly round in shape. They all stared at it in amazement.

'Ain't never seen one like it,' went on Ryan.

'Looks like a musket ball to me,' suggested Hunter. 'Like they used way back in the war.'

'Let's have it here,' ordered the sheriff, holding out his hand. He examined it closely and then shook his head. 'Naw, this is no musket ball. Too small. This is from a pistol. Old pistol, flintlock maybe.'

Nobody argued the point. Mike Heston had been all through the war and had a bayonet scar on his arm to prove it. They stood in silence, eyes flickering between the ball in the sheriff's hand and the bloody forehead of the

14

man it had done to death.

'I don't get it,' said Hunter at last. 'Who would use a gun like that? Old Civil War thing, ya reckon?'

'Could be older,' answered Heston, shrugging. 'The ball don't seem jest like them that I've seen. Might be from the war, though. At the start they was usin' all kinds of guns.'

'Couldn't it be that it's been in that tree for a long time – maybe since the war?' suggested Cal, and immediately regretted it as Ryan scowled at him.

'No, sirree, I told ya the break in the bark was fresh!'

'OK, so we're lookin' fer a feller with an old pistol,' decided Heston. 'I guess that's some kind of a start. What about tracks? Anything to go on?'

'Plenty of tracks around,' replied Hunter. 'Place is used all the time. Nothin' to pick out though, except Mr Valdes' sharp heels from them boots. He walked up the trail a little way after crossing the grass.'

'Out for a little Sunday evening stroll, heh?'

'Could be.'

'Well, we'd better see to him now. Best if his wife doesn't ever see him like that. Need to bring in Crawley. Say, Pinky, you know the undertaker's place in Baxters, don't ya? Why don't you ride into town and fetch Phil Crawley? Don't tell him nothin' except there's a body. Since we're lookin' for some polecat with an old gun it might help if we kin catch him with it before he gets time to get rid of it.'

Pinky had been standing a little way up the grassy slope, staring much of the time at Valdes, while listening to the conversation. He jumped slightly at hearing Heston speak to him and then nodded and went to his borrowed horse. He seemed suddenly nervous, much more so than he had appeared all morning. His eyes had a scared look. He mounted up without speaking or glancing again at the lawmen and then turned the horse's head down the track. They watched him disappear slowly around the nearest bend and then looked again in surprise as he reappeared almost instantly.

'Mr Heston.' He held in his fidgeting horse within a couple of yards of the sheriff, glancing out of the corners of his eyes and never quite catching the curious stare of the lawman. 'I got somethin' to say. It was when ya started on about that old gun – the old flintlock. I seen somebody with one of them . . .'

'You have? Well, out with it, Pinky. We need to know and the quicker the better.'

'It was nobody who lives around here. Thing is, well, I ain't supposed really to say . . . Mr Valdes, he told me straight not to tell nobody about them.'

'About who? Come on, Pinky, there ain't time to waste.'

'Them riders. The Mexican fellers. Three of them, well four, one time.'

'You seen them? More than once?'

'Sure. Thing is, I been workin' out in the woods other side of the hill. Been markin' out some trees that Mr Valdes wants felled to sell over at Carlune where the agent's lookin' fer straight timber. Anyhow, one day about a month ago, I was lookin' around there and I seen them three riders, Mexicans, straight up from over the border by the look of them, hard-lookin' men too, just riding real slow through the woods. Then I seen Mr Valdes. He comes down the trail and starts speaking to them real friendly. Sounded like Spanish. I couldn't understand any of it and they was talking low, anyhow. Then they all shook hands and they turned around and rode out faster than they had come in.

'Then I yells out "Howdy" to Mr Valdes and he was as mad as hell to see me, only I told him I was just carrying out his orders and sure wasn't

17

spying on him. So he tells me to keep my mouth shut about them riders who were just business friends of his and didn't figure on havin' their business spread all over the territory. So I did what he said and kept quiet or else, I reckoned, I would soon find myself out of work.'

'So, what about them Mexicans?'

'Well, I saw them again another time, only I kept my head down so that Mr Valdes didn't see. Then just about three days ago, they were here again, talkin' to Mr Valdes. I was in the woods and I heard their voices and then sees their horses hitched outside that broke-down old cutter's shed. I wasn't spying on them, really I wasn't, Sheriff, but I heard them arguing a bit, not fierce but kind of forceful-like, but then they all comes out, Mr Valdes and four Mex. Then they shook hands again and went away. I just kept down low in the thickets in case Mr Valdes sees me.'

'You think them Mexicans have got somethin' to do with this murder?' Heston nodded thoughtfully. 'Well, you could be right but . . .'

'Mr Heston, one of them had a real old gun – a pistol – in his belt. I never seen one like it, except in a picture-book. It was so queer-looking, all fancy-carved in silver and black, that I couldn't help lookin' at it. Long barrel, too, fer a pistol, with a big heavy butt. So, when I heard what ya said, well, it seems to fit.'

'Don't it just!' exclaimed Ryan.

'You said it!' agreed Hunter.

'This was three days ago?' put in Heston, cautiously, 'and they weren't any local Mex?'

'Nothin' like them. These guys were from over the border and they weren't poor like the sweatbacks who work around here, no sirree! They had pretty good clothes and fine sombreros and good horses, and they had rifles and six-guns.'

'And this old pistol, too, heh?'

'Spanish pistol, Mr Heston.'

TWO

Nobody else had seen the Mexican riders around the Valdes place, or if they had, they were keeping quiet about it. The Hispanics and Negroes and poor whites who worked the fields claimed always to have their heads down and never to have seen anything of any riders or much of Mr Valdes, who only rode out about once a day to see how the work was going. As a boss, he was all right, but he expected a good return for every cent he paid out in wages, and did not pay anybody for sightseeing.

At the house there was no information either. Mrs Valdes was too distraught to speak to anybody, but sent a message, through Maria, that she had never seen any Mexican riders and knew nothing of any of her husband's business deals. Maria said she would attend to the funeral arrangements, but knew no more than

21

did her mother. She spoke briefly in this manner to Heston but spared no more than the faintest of smiles for Cal when he expressed his sympathy. She was extremely withdrawn and tense and seemed anxious to avoid his company. That he found a little hurtful but he felt that he understood it. He knew that she had been devoted to her father and must be going through a torment of grief, although she obviously refused to allow herself to give way entirely to it. Only once, when he glanced over to the house from some distance away, did he see her in tears as she stood near a window. At that, his anger grew intense as he thought of the low-down skunk who had committed such a cowardly murder and he vowed revenge.

'Mr Heston,' he said, as he rode beside the sheriff towards the wooded hillside. 'I want to go with ya on this trail. Let me come with the rest of your posse. I got a real interest.'

'Yeah?' Heston looked at him curiously but with understanding. 'Well, so be it, but don't let your personal feelings get in the way. The law's only as good as the men who represent it.'

They searched around for tracks and found them in the soft earth of the woods, but they vanished soon enough out in the open where the dust blew across the trail and the ground had been trampled by the passage of hoofs and feet as men had gone about their daily tasks.

'Three days, heh,' grunted Heston to himself, 'but somebody came back on Sunday. Some feller who wasn't seen this time even by Pinky. Maybe with murder already in his mind or maybe not.'

'Could have been another argument,' suggested Ryan. 'Only this time it got serious.'

'Hellish serious,' agreed Abe Hunter.

By the time the undertaker arrived to attend to Juan Valdes, a posse had been gathered together, and were riding to the farm. They were a mixed bunch but mostly men who had acted as deputies before and knew what was expected of them. They all were well armed and well mounted and carried food and blankets for a chase that might last for weeks. All were deeply angered at the news of the murder, as Valdes had been a man generally well respected.

'Well, where to, Sheriff?' asked Will James, the local farrier. 'Pinky tells me there ain't even any tracks left by them polecats.'

'Mexicans would head south, sure as hell!' shouted Puppy Grant, straight from the livery stables. 'Let's git after them!'

'All right, fellers, we jest have to take this

slow and easy to start, and the less yelling the better, seems to me,' growled Heston, already irritated. 'Ken, you got pretty good eyes. You ride ahead and see if you kin pick out tracks of maybe three horses all bunched together or one lone horse that started off fast. We'll take the south trail, sure enough, far as Three Pines, if we don't git no better lead before then.'

There were no tracks that Ken Ryan, even with his sharp eyes, could pick out with any certainty. The trail to the south led through increasingly barren land, hot and dusty and rock-strewn. For miles there was nothing to be seen but this rugged landscape, baking under a pitiless sun. The country was not unfamiliar to them but it was a trail that none would have taken out of choice. Once in a while they came across men heading north, farm hands of Mexican blood, riding mules and leading others, heavily laden. Heston always stopped and asked them who they had seen on the trail but they had seen nobody except men like them-selves. It was only when they arrived in the late afternoon at a tiny adobe town that they learned that a small group of horsemen answer-ing the description had passed some days earlier. They had stopped for a drink at the downbeat saloon and the barman remembered them as the only strangers he had seen in weeks. He had no idea who they were or where they were going but he thought they had mentioned Snake Pit in their conversation – a little of which he could not avoid overhearing as he put out the glasses.

'Snake Pit?' mused Will James. 'That's east of here, ain't it? Damned, stinking, half-dried-out river ...'

'East and north,' grunted Heston. 'So they ain't heading back to Mexico. At least, not right now.'

They reached the desert country of Snake Pit later next day.

'Ain't come too soon fer me,' growled Hunter. 'This is like hell.'

'Looks like an Injun up there ahead,' indicated Ryan.

The Indian sat nearby the trail, prodding a stick into the ground in search of edible roots. He was clad in a dirty blanket and tattered white-man's pants, held up by a piece of rope. A battered black hat shaded his swarthy features, which were heavily lined and aged, with the dried-out look that comes from a life spent under the sun. He glanced at the group of horsemen with narrowed dark eyes which held a hint of suspicion, and hovered on the edge of fear.

'You seen any men ridin' by here?' asked Heston. 'Men? *Hombres*? *Sombreros grandes*?'

'*Sí.*' The answer came promptly in a husky tone which fell immediately into silence.

'Well, where are they? Where did they go?' Heston had grown more and more impatient with every hour of the hot day. '*Hombres*?' he waved his arms in a gesture of search. 'You say, quick, pronto!'

He touched the butt of his rifle as it hung in his saddle boot as if in threat. The Indian noted the movement but gave no sign of concern. His mouth spread into a grin of bad teeth and tobacco-stained saliva.

'You got whiskey?'

'No whiskey.'

'*Dinero*? Money? You got a dollar?'

'No money!' rasped Heston.

Ryan caught the Indian's attention and pointed to the pack-horses and then to his mouth, making eating gestures. The Indian seemed to get the idea. He straightened up as far as his bent, misshapen body would allow, and then shuffled off, making a sign with his crooked fingers for them to follow him. He moved with surprising speed in spite of a crippled leg, using his stick as a kind of rough crutch to propel him on his way. They followed cautiously, keeping their eyes open for trouble, well aware of the possibility of an ambush. His speed of progress was exactly wrong for the horses, a walk was too slow and a trot too fast, and they had to keep changing pace in order not to overtake him.

After about an hour of uneasy travel, they rounded an outcrop of rock and saw the ground flattening out ahead. Some distance away they could see twisted, gnarled trees and a glint of water. There was also the flash of red and blue clothing and a movement of some kind amid the trunks and low-hanging branches. Heston held up a hand to bring the party to a halt and stared hard, squinting against the lowering sunlight. In that second, a figure appeared from behind rocks to the right-hand side, not far in advance of themselves.

It was a horseman wearing a wide sombrero and a bright jacket. He stopped in surprise on seeing them, drawing in his horse so that it almost shied away. Another similar figure appeared just behind him. For the briefest of moments they held quite still, then it seemed to Cal, from his position just to the rear of Heston, that the Mexican caught sight of the sheriff's glistening star and was startled by it into taking action.

The man went for a gun at his belt. He was quick and it appeared in his hand as if by magic. The shot rang out and Heston gave a sudden yelp of pain and reeled in the saddle. Then he was down, one foot caught in a stirrup as his horse doubled around in alarm. A shot from the second Mexican hit Puppy Grant and he fell like a sack of grain with no sound reaching his lips.

For all their watchfulness, the posse was taken completely by surprise. Their eyes had been on the men down by the river and they had had no time to react to the sudden appearance of these two Mexicans. Now, with two men hit and horses milling about, their reaction was still too slow and those who went for their guns fired in haste and with little aim. In the confusion, the Mexicans turned and rode pell-mell towards their comrades in the trees, bullets from the posse flying wide.

Those Mexicans a little further off were leaping for the saddle and within seconds had mounted. There seemed to be only about three of them and, as they were joined by their countrymen, they turned and splashed through the shallow waters of the almost dried-up stream beside which they had been resting.

The posse gave chase, dismayed by the sudden loss of Heston and Grant, but confident in their numerical superiority. All were angry at what they saw as a treacherous attack. Some fired their rifles as they rode and Cal saw a Mexican fall. He himself was near the van of the thundering force, six-gun in hand, fierce in his determination to exact vengeance.

How he became separated from his friends, he was not sure, but the Mexicans were spreading out as they went, each seeming to be concerned only with his own survival, and Cal found himself pursuing a man with a dark sombrero who rode hunched low and turned his horse with the agility of a coyote through the scattered stones of the riverbank. Soon they had left all sign of the river behind them as the man led the way uphill amid shifting scree and tumbling pebbles.

As they rode, Cal became aware that the sounds of battle had receded and that he had followed a baffling route through the rugged landscape. His determination to catch up with the fleeing Mexican remained unabated but the man was very well mounted on a small, strong horse evidently well used to this kind of territory. His own horse was flagging after the long hot journey of the day and could not keep up with the savage demands now made upon it.

Its breathing became more and more laboured as it slithered and stumbled over the bad ground. The Mexican disappeared over a rise. Cal swore under his breath. He pressed in his spurs, hating to force the animal but wild in his desire to get to grips with the enemy. The horse bounded uphill, as if making one last desperate effort, then something went beneath it. Boulders moved, an avalanche of small stones poured under its hoofs, and horse and rider teetered and then fell heavily down the steep slope to one side.

Cal came to with the feeling that his skull had been crushed. Pain seemed to grind through his brain like a turning millstone. At first all was dark, then he became slowly aware of the searing heat upon his face and he forced his eyes open only to close them again quickly to shut out the blaze of sun which threatened to blind him.

He lay still, trying to figure out to what extent he had been injured. He had taken a severe blow on the head. That was evident. Spasms of pain shot up his left arm but he knew that it was not beyond movement. Apart from that, only aching muscles told him of his bruised body. He remembered the desperate ride and the wild fall, so his mind seemed unaffected. He could still think straight, thank God!

Thinking told him that many hours had passed. The sun was blazing with all the ferocity of noon and he remembered with clarity that the sun had been dropping for the western horizon when they had come across the Mexicans. The light had been shining in their eyes, putting them at a disadvantage in the fight and, no doubt, turning Heston's star into a warning beacon in the eyes of the bandits.

Something touched his foot and then drove into his side. It was sharp and hard. He opened his eyes again, twisting this time to turn his face from the sun. The old Indian sat there, rooting-stick in hand, eyes sharp and slightly malevolent.

'No dead?'

He could not answer. His mouth seemed as dry as the surrounding dust and sand. The stick poked again, this time stirring embers of anger. He frowned and attempted to push himself up on his elbows but pain defeated him and he sank back as if exhausted.

Other faces appeared, dark and intense. Three faces, all Indian. Two squaws, old and

gnarled-looking, and an old man under a droop-
ing thatch of grey hair. They stared at him for
several minutes, then one of the squaws smiled,
showing wide gaps between teeth. She pushed
the stick aside, at the same time holding up a
pacifying hand at its owner. She said something
in a guttural tone and made a motion to her
mouth.

He was given a drink of water from a skin. It
tasted alkaline and foul but it relieved his
thirst a little. He felt slightly better and pushed
himself up again, this time on his left elbow,
and looked around. His horse lay dead some
yards away, neck broken. The slope they had
tumbled down stretched up behind it. There
was a long rip in the animal's side and its liver
was stretched out on a stone and had been cut
into strips. The Indian with the stick had a
piece in his mouth.

The squaw stretched out a bloody hand and
offered a piece to Cal. He shook his head, his
face showing his disgust. She shrugged and
turned away. The other squaw offered a small
basket containing grasshoppers, still living, and
a dead mudskipper that had waited too long for
the rains. This, he guessed, was their normal
diet. The horse liver was an unexpected treat.
He again shook his head and this time he saw

the old Indian with the stick scowl.

Cal knew well enough that to refuse the food was an insult to Indian hospitality but he could not bring himself to attempt to eat it. Then he saw the old Indian lift up the gun.

It was Cal's own rifle. Still scowling, the Indian pointed it at Cal's chest. He was obviously angry that the offer of food had been rejected with such disdain. He pulled the trigger as Cal squirmed but the safety catch was still on, and there was nothing but a menacing click. The Indian tried again and then examined the gun more closely, his crooked old fingers fiddling with the catch. This time, it might well happen. Cal was about to call out for grasshoppers or raw liver when he saw a small pile of roots lying on the ground nearby. He indicated them and pointed to his mouth and a squaw passed one to him. He ate it with every pretence of enjoyment, as the rifle was lowered, then looked up to see a Mexican walking slowly towards him.

The man was not a *señor*; not a Mexican with any claim to riches or any place in society as the visitors to the Valdes place had been described. He looked dirty and unkempt and his clothes were old and the worse for wear. There was a revolver at his belt and a long knife in his boot.

He was a youngish man with a neglected moustache which hung over his mouth. His dark eyes were trained upon Cal as he drew near and they were full of a mixture of curiosity and distrust. When he was within kicking distance, he shifted the old Indian with his foot and snatched up the rifle.

'You, gringo, you sheriff man?' The rifle was pointed into Cal's face and the safety catch was clicked off. This man seemed to mean business. He did not strike Cal as a man who liked unnecessary argument. 'You sheriff man, you say quick.'

For a moment, Cal hesitated. It seemed to him that to admit to being a sheriff's man would be to invite the bullet waiting there in the rifle chamber in front of him. To deny it, on the other hand, would just be a worthless lie, which would soon be seen for what it was, and would be a contemptible denial of his position in all of this. He knew which side he was on. In his mind, he saw Maria's face as she had smiled at him before this tragedy began to unfold, and he knew he could speak only the truth and set himself beside her and her dead father and against this bandit and his murdering friends.

'Yeah,' he answered, 'I am a sheriff's man.'

'Sure. Why you here?'

'We're investigating a murder. We are goin' to arrest the murderer.'

The dark eyebrows were raised.

'Sure. What murder? Who murder who?'

'Mr Valdes was murdered but I guess ya know that already!'

The dark head shook, bouncing the sombrero.

'Señor Valdes no dead. He come pretty soon.'

THREE

The rifle still pointed. Cal decided not to argue. If this man wanted to believe that Valdes was still alive then it would not matter for the time being. He might not know about it. Certainly, he did not seem like the type of man who had been seen talking to Valdes. He had the appearance of a follower, a man who takes orders without, perhaps, asking too many questions. It was possible, though, that he might know something about what was happening. This idea about Valdes coming away out into this wild territory? What could it mean?

'Is Mr Valdes coming here to speak to you?' Cal attempted to sound as if the question was almost a casual one, but without success. 'You got business with him?'

'You say Señor Valdes is dead.' The man's eyes were narrowed in deep suspicion. 'Now you

37

say maybe he have business. You pretty good damn liar, heh?'

Cal's head was still throbbing. He put one hand up to his hairline and gingerly felt the matted blood. Talking was hard. His every word seemed to thunder through his brain.

'It's all right ... I guess, maybe, I made a mistake ...'

'You make mistake? Sheriff make mistake to come here, shooting. We lose one good man dead. Big boss pretty angry. He take out your guts.'

Cal lowered his aching head on to his arm. The running fight came back to him and he wondered what the outcome had been. It seemed as if the Mexicans had not suffered further loss to judge by what this feller had just said. They had been scattering and it could be that the posse had broken into small groups and might have got the worst of it in the individual combats which could have followed. He hoped, though, that he had been the only one foolish enough to ride out into trouble on his own. There was no doubt, anyway, that they had made a bad start. God, he hoped that Heston was all right ... and Puppy too ... but there had been something about the way they had gone down....

38

"You come see Señor Ibarra. Maybe he give you bullet or hang you up pretty quick.' The moustache-shaded mouth was suddenly grinning. 'You lucky I come. Hungry Indian maybe eat you – after horse!'

Cal stared into the barrel of the rifle and then made an attempt to rise. His head spun and he fell back, jarring his strained arm. He grimaced in pain. The rifle was thrust into his chest and then withdrawn. It was obvious even to his captor that he was unable to get up and walk. The Mexican cursed in Spanish and then straightened himself up and shouted at the Indians to give some help. They did so with every show of reluctance, prompted by fear of the gun and not by any concern for the helpless prisoner.

Withered and malnourished old arms gained hold on his clothing and waist and hauled him to his feet while he grunted with renewed pain. The four elderly Indians staggered to support him as he stumbled forward. He was only dimly aware of his surroundings as his feet sought to make clumsy progress through the stones and shifting dirt. The rifle was again prodding into his back and loud shouting and cursing accompanied him on his way.

Then the smell of hot animal hit his nostrils

39

and he found himself beside a mule. He held on to its back with his good hand and struggled to regain his senses. His vision cleared enough for him to see that there was a line of mules stretching along a narrow track.

'*Burro! Burro!*' The Indians were growling at him like so many dogs and the rooting-stick struck him across the shoulders. 'Up! Up on *burro!*'

He obeyed slowly, hauling himself up a little way by gripping on to the short, wiry mane and then he was being pushed roughly from behind. There was no saddle and only a short strap from the head-harness to hold on to but he gripped instinctively with his knees and in a moment felt the beast move forward.

Gradually, his head cleared a little and he saw that there were three mules ahead of him, led by a rider who looked like a young Indian or half-breed to judge by occasional glimpses of his heavy nose and dark skin. Behind, he knew by sounds that there were more mules and that one of them was ridden by the Mexican who had captured him.

There followed a long, slow ride through the heat and dust of afternoon. It seemed to him that they were making their way northwards or north-east as the heat of the sun beat relentlessly upon his back and neck.

They made no stop for rest. He heard the Mexican drink from a flask of some sort as he rode; the rider ahead chewed steadfastly upon tobacco but no refreshment was offered to Cal. To his great relief the sun fell at last behind towering bluffs and they continued for another hour in starlight and a cooling breeze. Then they saw deeper shadows ahead and a half-concealed flicker of light. As they approached there came a challenge in Spanish from out of the dark and the rider to the front of the column, almost invisible now to Cal, answered with some password that meant nothing to the young deputy.

Then they were riding slowly through a gap between the bulging shadows of covered wagons set out in a big square. Within this space screens of canvas had been set up which gave good concealment to several camp-fires and the smell of cooking floated though the night air. Here and there a shielded lantern gave some little light in the interior of a wagon and vague figures moved but without sound.

Cal was astonished. He had not expected to see anything like this. He had believed that the posse had been on the trail of some little band of Mexican bandits but here it seemed to him

41

were wagons enough to carry supplies for an
army. The number of fires suggested a considerable number of men and in the background he
could see the dim movement of mules and
horses tethered in orderly lines as if in prepa-
ration for a continued campaign in the morning.

His mind leaped to the notion that this was
part of an army – perhaps the vanguard of some
vast army now gathering on the border ready to
invade Texas and to win it back for the Mexican
government. The idea filled him with amazement and dread, but he had little time to think
before rough hands dragged him from the mule
and into the light of the nearest fire.

There were Mexicans here in plenty, rough,
ill-dressed men, bearded and moustached,
drinking steaming liquid from metal mugs and
chewing lumps of black bread. Those nearest to
him stopped eating and stared with suspicion
and hostility. The word 'gringo' passed from lip
to lip. One man drew a gun from its holster.

The Mexican who had captured Cal held up a
hand as if to calm them. He spoke rapidly,
seeming to explain something of the situation
to them and then asked for Señor Ibarra. Where
was Señor Ibarra? They shrugged and spread
their arms and some pointed into the distance.

Then somebody mentioned Salas. It seemed to Cal that Ibarra was not here but Salas was not far away. Maybe over the other side of the camp. Why not speak to him about the gringo?

Cal's Mexican captor was more than a little irritated. He swore and spat on the ground and looked longingly at the steaming cauldron by the fire. Then he pushed Cal from the firelight with the menacing rifle and drove him through the deepening shadows towards the wagons on the other side of the square. Here they came to a wagon which did not look any different from the others except that three sentries stood beside it. They snapped out a challenge and then an order and Cal's captor threw his rifle to the ground. One of the sentries rapped the stock of his gun against the shafts of the wagon and then spoke with much respect to the face which appeared from behind the canvas door-way.

There was a long hesitation while Cal was scrutinized as carefully as the dim light would allow, then came another order and Cal was prodded into clambering up on to the wagon and into its lit interior.

His eyes took a minute or two to become accustomed to the glare of the lamp but then he made out a tall, lean man with jet-black hair and long moustache. His eyes were unusually narrow and stared with an intensity which seemed to suggest difficulty in seeing past the aquiline nose. The man was well dressed in the Mexican fashion and wore silver rings on both hands. He was seated now upon a tiny camp-bed which was the only object in the wagon apart from a fine sombrero hanging from a hook and a long rifle nearby. There was a strange emptiness about the wagon, as if Señor Salas scorned all possessions except those he considered essential for his survival or for his fine appearance.

The narrow eyes stared long and hard at Cal who stared back with as much boldness as his situation made possible.

'*Su nombre? Ah, perdone* … What is your name?' The voice was low and almost gentle and the English was perfect with little trace of an accent.

'Cal Rogers.'

'The muleteer says you were with the sheriff in the skirmish yesterday. You are a lawman?'

'Only with this posse. I ain't a regular deputy.'

'This "posse" you mention killed one of our men yesterday for no reason.'

'The Mexican opened fire first.'

44

'He who shoots first usually comes off best.'

'Yeah. Maybe that's why Sheriff Heston and Puppy Grant were gunned down with no chance.'

The narrow lips twisted in recognition of the irony. The dark head nodded slightly.

'Why did this sheriff – this Heston – come here?'

'We're lookin' for a murderer.'

'Someone has been murdered?' Salas raised his eyebrows in exaggerated surprise. 'Who was the unfortunate victim?'

Cal hesitated. All of this situation was quite different from the way he or Heston or any of the others had imagined it to be. He needed to find out what was going on. Maybe he could ask some questions of his own.

'Listen, what's happening here? How is it that there's just about an army of you Mexicans come over the border into Texas? You don't have any right. When the US Army finds out, then all hell will be let loose. You need to think about what you're doing.'

'You are hardly in a position to be asking questions, my friend, or giving advice. I repeat – who was murdered?'

'Somebody you and your friends had dealings with.' Cal watched Salas's eyes as he spoke,

45

waiting for some revealing hint.

'Yes?'

'Mr Valdes ...'

'The muleteer reported that you had made such a claim but he thought you were lying. I need to point out to you that people who lie to me about important matters do not live for long – only long enough to regret it. If you tell me that you washed your dirty neck last week then I do not care if it is a lie or not but to tell me that Señor Valdes has been murdered is a lie of much greater consequence. Time seems to be running out for you, Rogers.'

'What kind of consequence?'

'Answer questions, do not ask them!' For the first time, Salas seemed to be on the edge of his temper. Real anxiety flickered behind the cold eyes. His ringed fingers drummed on the wooden frame of the camp-bed. 'Tell me about Señor Valdes. I want to know exactly what happened!'

'Do you not know already?'

A hand rose as if to strike out. Anger blazed in the lean face. Cal knew then that this man, Salas, truly was ignorant as to the death of Valdes. So it had been some other Mexican, almost certainly of the same band, who had been more directly involved in the negotiations

46

– whatever these had been – with Valdes. But this was no time to be stubborn. Salas was angry enough to condemn him to death right at this moment. Cal told the story of the finding of Valdes' body and how he had been shot and what little was known about his dealings with the Mexicans. He did not mention the ball from the old pistol and what Pinkie had said about the old Spanish pistol in the belt of the Mexican in the woods. That information needed to be held back for another time.

Salas seemed numbed with shock. For several minutes he stared at Cal and then turned away to stare fixedly at the floor of the wagon. It was apparent that he accepted the truth of the story and it was the kind of truth that comes to a man who suddenly knows that he has become lost in the desert. Something tragic loomed ahead of Salas. What that might be, Cal could not hazard a guess.

Eventually, the Mexican spoke again. His voice trembled slightly but his eyes, fixed again on Cal, were calm and deadly cold.

'I believe what you say, Rogers, but it is always possible that you are a very cunning liar. I have sometimes met men who can lie as if they were speaking the word of God. If you are one of those, then look out, for the fires of hell will light you to your grave.'

He got up from the camp-bed and stepped past Cal to the door. There he had some words with the sentry and Cal was ordered to another wagon some little distance away. There he was attended by a Mexican in a black suit who said nothing at all but cleaned and examined his head wound and then applied a dressing and a bandage. His sprained arm was also strapped up and the man went away without a backward look. Afterwards, soup and coffee and some bread were brought to him, and he ate eagerly, suddenly aware that he was ravenous with hunger. He fell asleep very quickly, watched by a sentry at the door.

He was awakened by the snorting of mules as they were harnessed to wagons and by wheels beginning to churn over the stony ground. His sentry had been replaced by another who was engaged in a shouted conversation with other men outside the wagon. Soon, this wagon too was hitched to its team of four mules and a driver leaped to the buckboard and swung them around to pull to the north. The wagon moved with ease for it made a light enough load for four strong beasts and Cal saw through the edge of the canvas that the other wagons each had a strong team and were already making good progress.

That was strange. Why such strong teams for light wagons? The answer came to him at once; the wagons were empty for the time being but were expected to be fully loaded on the return journey.

He pondered over this as they trundled on their way in a long column. He could see now that his first guess that this was part of an army had been wrong. What he had seen convinced him that most of the men present were muleteers, like the man who had taken him prisoner, and although they were all armed, they were probably not trained as fighting men. He had seen a number of others, well mounted, who looked like irregular cavalry, but could only guess at their strength. This was not an invasion so much as an expedition. But for what purpose? What had these Mexicans come all this way to fetch? Gold? Not with all these wagons. What else could be of such value to them as to make all this worth while?

It could only be arms – guns – perhaps to fight in some insurrection in their own troubled country!

He moved forward a little in the wagon to get a better view until the sentry warned him with a glare to come no further. Nevertheless, he could now see past the driver to some part of the rough trail ahead. There were other wagons blocking off most of the view but he could see a man sitting on a stationary horse watching the column go by. He was tall and strong-looking and mounted on an excellent horse. As they drew closer, Cal noticed that he had a small black beard and deep brown eyes that seemed somehow on fire. He was staring straight into the wagon as if interested to catch a glimpse of the prisoner. On his hip he carried a six-gun and from another holster in his belt there protruded the black-and-silver butt of an old pistol, elaborately carved....

'Señor Ibarra!' greeted the muleteer, removing his hat in a gesture of great respect.

The Mexican leader acknowledged the greeting with a curt nod of the head, but his eyes were upon Cal as the wagon trundled by. Cal met the fiery gaze and watched it change to an expression of deep trouble, tortured and weary, like that of a man carrying a heavy burden, but the voice when it came was even, though full of menace.

'So, Texan, you bring me news that fills my heart with despair. We go forward upon our business and if you have lied, then joy will return to us, and we shall take much pleasure in having our gentle muleteers tear out your lying tongue! Say no more at this time. We shall see what today and tomorrow brings and then every grain of truth will be dragged from you. Meanwhile, pray God to give you guidance!'

'And you!' answered Cal, angrily, as the Mexican turned away and put spurs to his horse so that he was soon overtaking the head of the column.

So, there goes the murderer of Juan Valdes, thought Cal, still carrying the murder weapon, and his mind playing some double game, for it seemed obvious that Valdes had much to do with the future plans of this Mexican expedition. That had been apparent from the reaction of Salas, and also the muleteer had said that Valdes was expected to come to them, or to meet them somewhere.

What, then, would happen when Valdes failed to rise from the dead? His murderer could expect nothing else, but the pretence must continue and Ibarra had promised to drag the truth from Cal, well knowing that the truth could not be admitted to.

FOUR

Maria stood in her father's room with the letter in her hand and listened for any sounds in the house. Her mother, she knew, was in the kitchen, consumed with grief, going through the motions of her daily tasks, while Sebastian sat, eyeing her dully, as he slopped his midday meal into his mouth.

It was not likely that she would be disturbed. Her mother would not seek her out to converse with her for there was little of feeling or trust between them and hardly a word had been spoken since her father's death. That canyon of their minds had always existed, with her mother and the poor, pathetic Sebastian on one side and she and her father on the other. Even so, she did not feel that she could stay much longer where she was and she had already read enough to understand her father's situation.

That same morning she had collected from the undertaker some items which Juan Valdes had in his possession when he died; his side-gun and holster, a little money, and the keys. She had recognized the keys of his safe as soon as they had been given to her. At the same time she remembered how he had stalked quickly into the house a few days ago and had gone straight to his room, without as much as a greeting to his wife or daughter, and then had come the sounds of the safe door being opened, something of some weight being pushed in, and then the keys turning swiftly.

Maria had felt the secrecy which had surrounded her father's actions and had thought too of the glimpse she had had a week earlier of two Mexicans riding away from the woods just before Juan returned from his supervision of the farm.

Now it all fitted together. There was the letter in Spanish making some final arrangements for the transfer of all the money in the leather bag which she now held in her hands. There was also the crude map with its indications of Flint's Peak and the Dust Bowl Valley. There was also an unstated threat of danger and a demand from her own heart that she must now take her father's place in all this and finish what he had begun.

She recognized the need to move quickly. The time of the arranged meeting was not far off and, worse, that posse led by Mike Heston was riding into something that he did not understand and complete disaster could be the only result.

With that thought she left the house quickly and quietly, with the bag partly concealed under her coat, and mounted the horse on which she had just returned from Baxterville. She rode out across the fields to look for Billy Crowfoot. She found him, as expected, weeding in the upper field and he took off his black hat deferentially so that his bronzed Indian features caught the full glare of the sun.

'You know the Peyote country pretty well, Billy?'

'Sure. I know.'

'You could lead me right through to Dust Bowl?'

He looked puzzled, then shrugged. 'Could lead anybody crazy enough to go.'

'That's me. Walk up to the stables, slow and easy.'

They rode out some time later on fresh horses and with a pack-animal carrying supplies. Maria had not spoken to her mother but had left a letter to say that she was visiting Garvon Crossing to tell her cousins the bad news. She did not know whether she could be believed but had a strong feeling that, because of the way things were, her mother might not care anyway. Not at this time. There was too great a shadow hanging over the household.

For the first few hours they followed the same trail as had the posse, but then Billy turned aside and went into the high, rugged land that drifted into barren desert, where there were no trails of any sort to be seen. He seemed to know his way by the shapes of towering rocks and ancient dried river-beds, winding snakelike ahead.

They went on for three days under the blasting heat of the sun and through the bitter cold of the nights, resting a very few hours before early light prompted them again into movement.

Then they reached the Dust Bowl Valley, spread out yellow and red before them. Far beyond, Flint's Peak jabbed into the sky.

Another half-day of travel brought them to a high ridge from which the land fell away below to coarse grass and a glint of water. Maria looked around carefully to get her bearings and compare them with the crude map. It seemed to

56

her that they were just about on target.

'There, Billy,' she said. 'See that hill? The one with the steep drop to the north? That's the place. Keep your eyes peeled ...' Her voice trailed off a little at the absurdity of the remark for Billy's eyes missed nothing. 'Best to see them before they see us.'

They saw the roofs of the wagons first and then the movement of animals, grazing nearby. Then they saw men standing guard, wide-brimmed hats leaving no doubt as to who they were.

They met Ibarra and Salas and some of their men coming out of the camp to meet them. Rifles were ready but were lowered as they drew near enough to be clearly seen. The Mexicans looked puzzled and then downcast as she told them who she was and of her father's death.

'We have been told this already,' said Salas dolefully, 'but we did not know for certain if it was true.'

'Who told you?' asked Maria, surprised.

'We have a prisoner from the sheriff's posse. He calls himself Rogers. You know him?'

'Very well.'

'There was a fight. They killed one of us. We think we killed some of them.'

'My God, I hope not! But Cal ... Cal Rogers ... is he all right?'

'He is uninjured – well, apart from small hurts.'

There was relief in her eyes. They saw it and understood.

'If we had known,' smiled Salas, 'that there was romance between this Cal and the daughter of Juan Valdes, I think we might have been more polite to him!'

Maria looked slightly embarrassed. 'There is business to be done,' she said abruptly. 'I have the money – your money. I am willing to act as my father would have, although we have left it a little late.'

'Thanks be to God and all the saints!' exclaimed Salas. 'The money is safe? You have it with you? All in US dollars, changed from Mexican pesos?'

'Yes,' replied Maria, suddenly seeing the reasons for her father's frequent trips to various townships over the weeks, on 'matters of business' as he had put it.

'The gringos are still there,' put in Ibarra. 'Our scouts have seen them. They grow a little impatient, perhaps, but they still wait.'

'There is no trust between us,' said Salas. 'When they see that Valdes does not come, the

58

deal may well fall through.'

'If you wish I can take the place of my father,' offered Maria. 'I have letters to prove who I am. In the morning, I will go to meet with them. They must accept me as they would my father. I'll take Billy Crowfoot with me. They will not object to him.'

'What do you say, Señor Salas?' asked Ibarra. 'Can we allow this lady to ride into the lion's den?'

'Her father did no fear the soldiers. He saw no danger.'

'There is always danger.'

'There is also very much at stake.'

'For Mexico, then,' agreed Ibarra.

'For Mexico,' murmured Maria. 'My father's home country.'

'You will have an escort. We cannot permit you to go completely unprotected,' protested Salas.

'They will need to keep well back,' said Ibarra, 'but in case of trouble, you are right.' He looked straight at Maria. 'You are a brave lady. Might I ask why you do this? You, a Texan, born and bred?'

'Because to some extent, I sympathize with your cause,' replied Maria, 'but mostly it is because my father wanted it done.'

And he wanted to be well paid, thought Ibarra, but he was too polite to say so, although he made up his mind that he would honour that side of the bargain.

Cal was brought from his wagon shortly after Ibarra and his party had returned to camp. As he walked, still under guard, towards the leader's wagon, he could see that the wagons were positioned now near the edge of a steep hill and set into a defensive circle. There were more guards standing in readiness and the muleteers spoke in more subdued tones as if in expectation of an event of importance and probably of some danger.

When he saw Maria, Cal was astonished and then flooded with dismay How had she been made a prisoner? He had last seen her in her own home, although he had not spoken to her, and did not know for certain how much Heston might have told her about the crime and the objective of the posse. When she smiled at him now, and moved towards him with no suggestion that she was held as a captive, he was filled with amazement.

'Maria, why are you here? How did you come?'

'Billy Crowfoot led me. I may as well let you know, Cal, that I'm to act as go-between for Señor

Ibarra in this deal he has with the army ...'

'The army? It can't be the regular army. You're talking about guns, ain't ya? The army wouldn't do any kind of a deal in the middle of the goddamned desert and I'm pretty sure selling guns to the Mexicans like this is illegal! You can't mix yourself up in this, Maria!'

'My father was involved in it!' she answered, suddenly nettled, 'and I'll carry on as he left off. In any case, these men are fighting for their rights under an unjust government. Do they not deserve help?'

'How can we judge how unjust it is? This way, you're acting against the US government.'

'The same government that your elder brother got killed fighting against not so many years ago!' She faltered, sudden pity springing into her dark eyes. 'Look, I'm sorry I said that, Cal, but it's true.'

'That's all past! The war's over. We're all in the Union now. It ain't right what your father was doin', Maria.'

'I'm doing it.' Her voice was firm. Suddenly he saw the futility and the danger of his arguments. If she backed out now she would not live to tell the tale. Salas had let him know that nothing could stand in the way of this enterprise. He glanced at Salas, who stood staring at them with a faintly sardonic leer playing about his lips. Ibarra was nearby also. He seemed, in some ways, a different kind of man from Salas; slower of manner, less sharp, but he stood there with that old pistol still sticking out from his belt, looking at the daughter of the man he had gunned down, and without a trace of conscience.

Well, the posse had not ridden all this way to put down a gun-running operation. They had come after a murderer, and that murderer stood there within three yards with the murder weapon in plain view. He wondered if Maria had seen it and knew anything of its significance. Heston might have told her something, although he had insisted to his deputies that the peculiar nature of the weapon must be kept secret. It was iron-hard evidence that must not be lost to them, but maybe all that had now changed since they had lost two good men from Mexican bullets, one of them being Heston himself.

Why? The question came into his mind with renewed force as he looked at Ibarra. Why had he gunned down Juan Valdes? At first it had seemed the act of a Mexican bandit, determined on revenge for some wrong, real or imagined, or a failed attempt to lay hands on money. There had been much money involved in all this but not in any way that Heston could have imagined. The money had been with Valdes temporarily, as had been the Mexican plan, and it seemed that they had expected him to continue to act as negotiator with the arms suppliers. Why then kill him? What secret agenda did Ibarra have – or had there been another private deal with Valdes which had gone wrong and that swift, treacherous ball had been unleashed in a moment of anger?

But now was not the time to voice demands for answers to such questions. Maria, and he himself, were in the power of Ibarra and his followers and care must be taken with every remark made and every thought that might register in the face. He had already said too much in his argument with her which had been listened to with such attention.

'The American war has ended, Mr Rogers, but the Mexican one may be just beginning.' Salas was smiling but his eyes were cold. 'Señor Ibarra and I have our sacred duty to perform. Señor Valdes was helping us in this until his tragic death, over which we have already expressed our sympathy to his courageous and beautiful daughter. We trust that she has now persuaded you to her point of view?'

'My concern is for her. I don't like to see her put herself in such danger. If she is determined to go through with this then I want to be with her, as her bodyguard.' Cal uttered the words in a rush of genuine feeling as he looked at her. 'I ain't much interested in any Mexican war; it's you, Maria, that I'm thinking about!'

'You are romantic and gallant, Mr Rogers,' put in Ibarra. 'We approve of such qualities! What do you think of Mr Rogers as a body-guard, Señor Salas?'

Salas looked with close amusement at Cal's bandaged head and bound-up arm and nodded. 'Excellent, I am sure!'

'I agree,' said Maria. There was no amuse-ment in her voice, only a hint of resentment at their barely concealed contempt for Cal's offer. 'But he will need to be armed. Here, take this, Cal.'

She reached up to her saddle and brought down a gun belt and a Colt .44, which had belonged to her father. Ibarra put out a prevent-ing hand.

'In the morning, good lady. That will be early enough for this young man to be armed.'

They were brought to Ibarra's wagon and for a time it seemed that they were to be treated as honoured guests. They shared a meal with the two leaders and Ibarra did much of the talking, describing with enthusiasm the virtues of his native country. The subject of the death of Valdes was skirted round and barely mentioned, whether out of concern for Maria's feelings or for some other reason Cal was not certain. Ibarra had changed his clothing and the Spanish pistol was not to be seen.

Darkness had fallen when the little dinner party broke up, Salas pointing out that the *señorita* must be very tired after the rigours of her journey.

Maria was led off to the privacy of a wagon in a more isolated part of the camp and two trusted guards were placed outside to protect her from 'any possible danger', as Ibarra explained. The bag of money remained in his own wagon for safe-keeping. Meanwhile, Cal was brought back to the wagon he had travelled in and a sentry posted over it, so that he knew that he was as much a prisoner as he had always been.

He lay in the dark and peered again through the gap under the canvas side. From where he was, he could see the wagon of Salas not many yards away. There was a lamp burning inside which was at length extinguished, and a little later he heard Salas say something in a low

65

voice to the sentry who stood outside. The man went off into the dark and returned some minutes later, followed by two burly men. Cal had the impression in the starlight that both were bearded although he could not be sure. They moved with what seemed like particular caution, making no sound as they clambered into the wagon.

The lamp was not relit but Cal, by listening with great care, could just detect voices in murmured conversation. There was no way of telling what was said. No clear word reached him even in the still night air. Even the guard who was seated just inside the entrance to his own wagon seemed completely unaware and was already half-dozing.

At last the faint sounds were stilled and the two figures appeared again, stepping down silently from the shadows of the Mexican leader's wagon. One of them stopped for a moment and seemed to stare directly at Cal, who lay quite still, scarcely breathing, although he knew that he could not be seen.

The man stood immobile, as if deep in thought, seeming – as it seemed to Cal – to turn over in his mind the instructions of his leader.

Wondering what these instructions might be kept Cal awake for much of the night. When, at last, he was allowed to emerge from the wagon in the half-dark before daybreak and was given a mug of hot, black coffee, his mind was filled with a trepidation that he could not have explained.

His peace of mind was not helped at all when he saw Salas speak to a group of men who were preparing to mount their horses. He guessed that they were to make up a bodyguard and were all hand-picked by Salas himself.

They set off in the early dawn with the sun breaking across the mountains to the east. The land ahead fell away into low hills under brownish grass and scrub, broken here and there by rocks and scree and the rough courses of dry stream-beds.

Billy Crowfoot rode some distance to the fore, his sharp eyes scanning the landscape. Maria and Cal rode in the company of a young Mexican who had been assigned to them in case of trouble. His presence made conversation difficult as they were uncertain as to his knowledge of English. It had occurred to Cal to say something to Maria about Ibarra and the pistol so that she might be forewarned that she was dealing with a vicious murderer and not the polite and gentlemanly patriot that he made himself out to be. But there was no opportunity of broaching the subject. To do so would almost certainly lead to an immediate, deadly reaction. It must wait. This business had to be gone through first and then he would figure out what to do next.

He was well aware, also, that the company of Mexican riders were not far behind them, just out of sight but within earshot if things began to go wrong. Salas had insisted on this reserve bodyguard whose duty it was to save the money in the event of an attempted double-cross, but with less concern, Cal guessed, about the lives of those at present in charge of it.

They reached the foot of a winding, narrow valley and followed its course between steep slopes. It went on for about a mile before they saw a man on horseback some distance ahead and caught the sudden flash of a telescope in the sun.

'Three men,' said Billy.

They did not rein in their horses but went on at a slow pace. As they approached, Cal made out that the man on horseback was dressed in a faded blue uniform of the Union Army but wore a Confederate cap.

'So much for the regular army,' he muttered to himself. 'Bunch of renegades or deserters, still on the run.'

The two other men that Billy had noticed were standing a few yards further back with rifles sloping but ready for use. They also were dressed in remnants of uniform though one wore a pair of buckskins.

'Hold it jest there!' The man with the Reb cap spoke slow and easy but with just enough authority to indicate that he meant what he said. 'Thet's near enough.'

They were close enough now to observe every detail of the man. He in turn scrutinized them with what seemed like an even greater interest.

'Didn't expect no wimmin,' he said at length. 'An' where's Valdes?'

'My father is dead,' replied Maria. 'I have come in his place to do business. I can prove who I am by this letter I have with me, if you wish.'

'No need.' The soldier was looking at her narrowly, with a glint of admiration. 'You've got somethin' of your daddy's looks, though a damned sight purtier! Your paw dead, though, huh? How come?' He grinned suddenly and joked, 'Bullet in the back, eh?'

Marie did not reply for an instant, then she said, 'He's dead, that's all you need to know.'

'Yeah?' The man looked surprised but unabashed. 'Valdes dead, huh? Well, I sure am sorry to hear it.' The corners of his mouth twisted again into a half-grin. 'He and I were buddies in the old days. In the same unit in the war. Always got on swell together, him givin' the orders and' me takin' them. We was jest about starting to change thet.... Thing is, I went over to the Union Army after the war and I seed him sure lookin' down his big nose at me last time we talked hereabouts. But I guess it don't matter now. Since you're here, I kin talk to you, and I hope it makes sense. First, though, why did ya bring along this here Injun dirt an' the sweatback an' the hospital case?'

'I'm here to negotiate the final deal, not answer your foolish questions and insolent remarks!' snapped Maria, eyes flashing. 'Let's get on with it.'

He looked at her closely, a flicker of admiration coming into his expression.

'Plenty of buck fer a mare,' he said, half to himself, then in a louder tone. 'You got the money? We can't do nothin' without the money. Your daddy tell ya thet?'

'It's here.' Maria patted her saddle bags. 'But I need to see the guns.'

'Yeah? It looked to Cal as if the man was about to break out into laughter and his own uninjured right hand crept nearer his holster.

70

'Well, well, sure, the guns ... you'll see them soon enough. Where's Ibarra an' Salas?'

'They have stayed behind in camp,' answered Maria in surprise. 'Why need they come? They trust me.'

'Your old daddy said he would fix it so thet they was here, right up in front. It was kinda part of the deal. It suited him better – more than us. But I guess it don't really matter, so long as you have the money. Let's look at it.'

'Let's see the guns.'

The man stared at her again. Cal read the expression in his eyes. It seemed to say – what a fine, spirited beautiful girl, and what a crying shame of waste!

FIVE

Cal's fingers were touching the butt of his side-gun. He sensed rather than saw the Mexican to his left do the same. The renegade soldier peered at them closely, the faintest of grim smiles touching his mouth, then the Reb cap shook slowly. 'All right, fellers, turn down the lamps.'

The Reb cap vanished backwards in a flurry of blood as the rifle bullet from somewhere behind Cal smashed into the man's forehead, toppling him from the saddle. The soldier in the buckskin pants fell, clutching his chest. In that same instant a bullet sang past Cal's head, tearing at his bandage. He knew almost intuitively that it was no mistake. That bullet had been intended for him as the others had been aimed at the soldiers. For the fraction of a second, he froze in fear, then he moved like lightning and threw out his strapped arm to clutch at the bridle of Maria's horse.

'Go! Go! Let's go!' He bawled like a madman, only too well aware of the acute danger, and both horses bolted forward, while the downed soldier's mount careered around them. He turned for the slope to the right, digging in his spurs cruelly in his urgency. There was no track, only spaces between stones under slippery grass, and wild hoofs scrambled. Both horses slobbered in panic as they were driven on.

Maria kept pace with him, leaning over her mount's neck, her face set. They rode at an angle across the gradient, pushing uphill as hard as the animals could go. Another bullet went by, splintering a rock only yards from them. At any second Cal expected the horrific impact of a bullet in his back. Every muscle and nerve was tense. His lips moved in silent prayer, incoherent and almost crazy.

Loose stones gave way beneath his horse, and it half-fell, slithering to one knee. He held on grimly, fighting to keep control while Maria pounded her way further up the slope. At that moment, head twisted, he glanced downhill towards the draw where the meeting had taken place. He saw what he had almost expected to see: more soldiers, about a dozen it seemed, lying amongst boulders and shooting back along the way he had come. At the far foot of the slope, the young Mexican who had been with them lay dead in the dirt. Beyond him, the small bodyguard of Mexicans who had followed them across country had dismounted and two lay in the open, writhing with their wounds. A third lay across a boulder, his head a goblet of blood.

Three or four others had taken cover and were exchanging shots with the renegade soldiers, amongst them a burly Mexican with a greying beard, who crouched behind a boulder, rifle firing. Their horses moved in panicky confusion behind them. One was a fine white beast, standing out from the rest. That was Salas's horse! Cal recognized it in the same instant as he urged his horse to rise. Surprise showed on his face even amid the fear. He had not expected that! Why should Salas, one of the top men, be with that tiny bodyguard? Then suddenly he knew – it figured! – it figured! ... but there was no time to think further ... time only to move, to ride like hell, for these rifles, from whichever side, had been ready to kill him and would bring him down at the first chance, whenever they could be twisted around in his direction away from the conflict in which they were at that moment engaged.

Scrambling hoofs passed above him, following the same path of flight but climbing with more success. Glancing up, he saw Billy Crowfoot, riding as if possessed by a demon and catching up fast with Maria.

Within a few more minutes, Cal realized to his own surprise and relief that they had put a ridge between themselves and the gunmen below. The firing could still be heard but the combatants could no longer be seen. There was no time, though, for rest, however brief. The need to put a long distance between themselves and the renegades was uppermost in their minds. Only Billy Crowfoot spoke, once, expressing what was in their minds already: 'Mexes soon all shot up! They git it bad!'

There seemed nowhere to go. The realization struck Cal all at once with callous suddenness. There was only barren hillside on the edge of the desert and enemies in the gullies and amongst the rocks. Nevertheless, they had no other prospect than to ride on, thankful still to be alive.

At first they rode along the crest of a broad hill, rejoicing silently in their hearts to have a level firm surface and to feel their horses make better progress. They had not gone far when the animals began to slow. That fierce climb had drawn on their reserves of energy and they could not go on at a fast pace even when the going was becoming easier. Then, one by one, the beasts came to a halt, lungs heaving, lather dripping from their muzzles.

'It can't be helped.' Maria was herself gasping for breath. 'They'll drop dead if we push them much further.'

They dismounted and stood holding bridles, while their eyes were inevitably turned back the way they had come. They were out in the open and they expected at any moment to see riders rise above the near horizon and bear down upon them.

'Where we go now?' asked Billy.

'North-east,' suggested Cal. 'That way we kin reach a township – Maples, maybe, or Sand Fall.'

'Too long way. We die of thirst first.'

'What do you mean?' Maria was staring at Cal, mystified. 'We must make our way back to the camp as best we can.'

He stared back at her, biting his lip, surprised that she had not understood what had happened back in that draw, although to him it seemed obvious.

'Maria, that was a deliberate ambush...'

'I know. I knew there was something when I looked into that man's eyes ... and then, when I saw the soldiers lying there spread out in the rocks, shooting. It must have been planned all along.'

'Not jest the soldiers, Maria. Sure they had it in for us. They were after the money without handing over no guns but these Mexicans had the same idea. They jest about blew my brains out from behind.'

'That must have been just an accident, Cal! They were shooting at the soldiers and you were nearly hit by a stray bullet. Thank God it missed you!'

'Maria, they started shooting when there was no need. They couldn't see into thet renegade feller's eyes like you could! Them soldiers wasn't ready to make their move but the Mexicans opened fire on them first chance they got!'

'Why?'

'To stop the money being handed over. That bunch of Mexicans that was supposed to be our escort never intended that the money would be passed over, but they waited too long. They should have finished us off before we got to the draw so as to get the money but they must have been held back a little on the trail—'

'Come on, Cal! Why should they do that? They're all in it together.'

'Salas was there. Why should he ride with that bodyguard? Did ya see his horse? No? Well, he was there!'

'Still, even if he decided at the last minute to ride with them that doesn't mean by itself that he's out to steal from Ibarra and the others! And as for the shooting – maybe they saw somebody raise a gun or perhaps they saw some of the soldiers crouching in ambush. You can't say for certain what they were thinking.'

'No, maybe not for certain, but it was all too pat for my liking. If the guns had been at the top of Salas's mind he would have waited, even jest for a few more seconds, to be sure that they were being double-crossed.'

'That might have been too late.'

'Maybe, but this was supposed to be too important a deal for them to come in shooting from the hip! It was supposed to have been all set up by your father. A double-cross should have been about the last thing on their minds.'

'Perhaps, but there was always the chance. That's why they sent a bodyguard ... but if Señor Salas was there, as you say, then maybe he has been killed.'

'Maybe, but somehow I doubt it,' answered

Cal. 'I guess he would git clear while his men were doin' the fighting. That's the way he seems to me.'

'Maybe he isn't as bad as you think!'

'I don't trust any of them, to tell ya the truth, Maria, and, as for Salas, especially after last night-'

'We need git movin'.' Billy Crowfoot interrupted the argument. 'We spend all this time talkin', we git our mouths shut up with bullets.'

They mounted up and moved on at a walk and then at a trot as the horses began to recover a little. They descended by degrees as the land fell away then Billy grunted a warning:

'Rider up there. Keep heads down.'

There was a man in a blue tunic riding well up the slope with his shoulders against the sky. He was looking ahead as if he thought they must have gained more ground than they had done. He carried a rifle sloped across his saddle bow and ready for use. His appearance now indicated that the gunfight was over and the Mexicans had got the worst of it, as Billy had thought.

'Come,' hissed Billy, 'low down, quick. No speak!'

They dismounted and coaxed the horses part

of the way down the steep hillside until the rider could no longer be seen. Cal drew his six-gun and Maria produced a small revolver. Billy had no weapon but a knife which he left where it was in his belt. All knew that a chase across this rough country on blown horses could result only in their being overtaken and shot.

They did not move until the occasional shouts which came to their ears had died away, then Billy motioned for them to move further down-hill. They led their horses with care, fearful that a careless slip could leave them with a crippled and useless mount. As the slope eased out Billy held up a hand.

'Plenty soldiers around. They search ahead then come back to look again more careful. We need lie low till dark.'

'Yeah, but where?' asked Cal. 'They can't miss us here, that's for sure.'

'We move fast and quiet,' answered Billy. 'Maybe we git chance..'

He led them along the narrow valley floor and then into a gully overhung with scrub and ancient sandstone. As he went, he seemed to search around for half-remembered clues, and nodded with some suggestion of satisfaction when he saw a sharp-edged rock and again, some time later, when the red sandstone gave way to a

81

yellower colouring. At length, he halted and motioned for them to follow him up the steep slope to the left and they saw him disappear into the rock face.

The cave mouth was narrow and concealed from below but was just spacious enough to allow for the entrance of a horse and they led the animals in one by one. Then Billy went outside once again and brushed away all signs of their ascent of the slope, using a branch of scrub for the purpose. The gully floor itself was hard and left little sign of their passage, although his sharp eyes had picked out traces of other horses, probably those of the soldiers, which had passed along it within the past few days. That made Billy feel more secure, as only the most skilled tracker could have distinguished between them.

It was the best that could be done and they were relieved to find themselves in the coolness of the cave which led in a winding corridor into the ancient rock.

'Come,' said Billy, 'there is another way out, up, up, but no good for horses. I show you in case ... well, maybe I git killed then you kin find it anyway. Here, this way.'

He struck a light and led Cal deeper into the cave. After a few yards, he stopped and pointed to the walls, a broad grin spreading over his rough features.

'Look,' he said, 'very good picture, heh? Good old Injuns here long time before white Texans or Mexes. Good old Injun time. No horses, no money, no guns. Plenty of good hunting. Everybody happy.'

The pictures were done in bright, natural colours, with figures of hunters armed with spears and bows. Wild bison and antelope roamed over a green landscape. It seemed like a happy place, sure enough, without all the so-called improvements brought by the white man.

'I guess you know this country pretty well, Billy, you've been here before?'

'Sure thing. When boy. We all live around here. Better country then, better Injuns too. We were stronger all them years ago. Now we don't seem to amount to much…. Now, well, what the hell, look at me. Work like a squaw in them fields all the time. Valdes place OK but it makes a man feel like a *burro. Comprende?*'

'Yeah,' answered Cal. It was the first time he had thought of it but he could see well enough what was meant, and he recognized in Billy's shaded eyes the expression of a man who had long since lost sight of any promising trail through life.

They did not climb the cramped, chimney-like tunnel that led at a sharp angle into the gloom. Billy just pointed out its entrance to them and said that it came out near the top of a ridge. It was a hard, rough climb but they could do it if they were trapped in the cave, and there was nothing else for it.

They returned to the cave mouth and kept a close watch. Some time in the afternoon three horsemen went by, looking with puzzled eyes at the trail. They were the same kind of renegade troopers who had lain in wait amid the rocks and had blasted the Mexicans. They looked angry and frustrated but determined. They went on past the cave and, much later, returned the same way.

When darkness fell, Billy said he was going out to do some scouting. If they were going to have any chance, they were going to have to go on horseback, but first, he must spy out the land from overhead. By this time, he reckoned, the soldiers would be lighting a fire for warm food and drink and maybe he could spot it, although he knew that they would have their scouts out also.

He vanished into the tunnel, leaving Maria and Cal staring at the dim, pale face of each other.

84

'You all right, Maria?' Cal asked, after some minutes of strained silence. 'I didn't mean to get you riled about Salas and that trap.'

'There was a trap but it was one set by the soldiers. As for Salas, I don't fully trust him either but I don't believe he is such a traitor. I'm going back to Ibarra to return this money. It's only right and it's what my father would have done if he had been here.'

Cal was silent for some minutes, staring out into the dim outlines of the rocks in the early starlight. What her father would have done? Not for the first time, he found himself reflecting carefully on Juan Valdes; a hard-working, decent man, concerned only to make his farm pay well enough to support his family. Now, though, mixed up in gun-running, seemingly in support of Mexican rebels who might – or might not – have a just cause. Cal could not make any judgement on that question but somehow it seemed a hell of a risk for a quiet, family man to take. Then, there was the other thing, the thing the guy in the Reb cap had mentioned before Salas's men blew out his brains. Valdes had wanted Ibarra and Salas there in the draw with him, although there was no reason for them to be there since he was entrusted with the negotiations. The feller had thought it a little strange but did not care much one way or the other, and Cal had seen in his eyes why it was of so little concern. It was the same thing as Maria had seen – the death sentence, which would pass out bullets instead of renegade guns, and take full payment just the same.

How much had Juan Valdes foreseen of that treachery? How much of its shape had been clear to him? Not all, that was for sure, since he had expected to walk away from it, but what had he imagined he could walk away with – and with whom?

But these were suspicions to which he could not give expression at this time – not to the trusting daughter of Valdes, sitting so close to him, and who had become so important in his own life. Such ideas must wait until they might be proved. Nevertheless, there was the other thing.

'Maria, you say that you're goin' back to Ibarra. I have to tell you this, Maria, and it ain't easy, but your father was killed by a ball from an old pistol. They reckon it was an old Spanish pistol, a hundred years old, maybe more. Ibarra carries one himself. I've seen it in his belt. He was seen with it near your house too, when he was there speaking to your father. Heston reckoned that if he found the pistol he would have the murderer. I don't know why Ibarra would have done that. Maybe it was a quarrel about the deal, who knows? But Ibarra was the man the whole posse was after before we got shot up.'

She stared at him through the half dark and then turned away her eyes. As she did so, he caught the look of a haunted soul within them.

SIX

No other word was said for some time. It was an uneasy silence that hung upon the air like some supernatural presence. Maria seemed deep in her own thoughts and he knew that these thoughts held her in a grip that he could not shake, desperate as he was to find something to say that might help her. When, at length, she spoke it was in a calm voice as though nothing had really been troubling her, although her question was a serious one.

'Cal, I suppose you still feel yourself to be a lawman in all this?'

He hesitated before he answered, not because of any doubt he might have had of himself, but because he felt that his reply could raise a barrier between them.

'Yeah, I guess I am at that, Maria. I was sworn in as a deputy before the posse set out and I'm still bound to it, along with Heston and Hunter and the others, I'm still looking for the man who killed your father.' He wanted to shout: *You don't seem so concerned about that, yourself!* but knew that he could not do so. She was vulnerable, too scared by something that he did not fully understand.

'All right, Cal, I ought to have known without asking. It was a stupid question.'

'Listen, Maria, we're in this together. You've got to trust me. We need to talk—'

'I don't want to talk any more, Cal, I'm tired. Leave it just now, all right?'

The silence again descended, then she said, almost casually, 'How are the horses?'

'Thirsty but rested, I guess,' he replied shortly.

They became aware of Billy Crowfoot approaching in near silence from the rear of the cave. He crouched beside them, breathing quickly but with little sound from his exertions.

'Soldiers all in camp,' he whispered.

'You've seen them, Billy?' asked Cal eagerly.

'Seed fire – two fire. Tents, wagons, all camp cosy,' he grinned in the half-light. 'Like Sunday-school picnic.'

'Yeah? Peaceful as that, is it?'

'Peaceful as grave.' There was something in

90

his voice that made Cal stiffen. It was as if there was something that the Indian was not quite sure of. 'You come see ... Miss Valdes very safe here for little while.'

'Sure, you go and check it out, Cal,' agreed Maria. 'We've been safe in here all day. Nobody is likely to come searching around here now.'

With some misgivings, Cal followed Billy into the recesses of the cave. The idea of leaving Maria even for a short time worried him but there was no doubt that she was safer where she was.

The climb up the chimney-like tunnel was difficult enough but held little danger for a fit man – or woman, come to that. It was narrow and contained many sharp corners but was not steep and rose fairly gently, for all its interior roughness, to the surface. They emerged on a stone-covered slope, almost on the edge of a sharp ridge. To one side, the ground fell away precipitously to the gully they had ridden along that day; on the other, there was undulating hillside which disappeared into the darkness.

Billy Crowfoot led on without hesitation up and over several little horizons of hill, each of which reared up in turn as if to block their progress. Then he held up a warning hand

91

against the night sky, and breathed sharply through his pursed lips.

Cal peered forward, his gaze following the now outstretched arm, and saw the glowing fire hanging in the dark.

It was not very far away. Something about its size told him that; although, as his eyes sought to make out more detail, he came to realize that it was bigger than most camp-fires. Unusually large, in fact. Also there was a second fire, not far in the background, of about the same size, and that one lit up the shape of a tent and part of the end-section of a wagon.

'Let's git nearer,' he hissed in Billy's ear, and the Indian nodded and sprang forward with an alacrity which suggested that he himself had already approached much nearer on his earlier mission.

They lay in the coarse grass of the lower hillside for some time, taking in as much of the scene as was possible in the starlight and the light of the fires. There seemed to be only three wagons and perhaps four tents of various sizes in the vicinity of the camp-fire. Also, there were the huddled forms of sleeping men, well wrapped up in blankets, and close enough to the flames to benefit from the warmth. Some mules and horses were ground-tethered in the shadows of the background.

The camp was in low ground where an old river valley, long since dried out, curved smoothly between rising rock. The higher, stony, gorse-covered banks of that ancient stream arose on both sides of the campsite as if to fence it in.

It was a bad place for a camp in a time of hostilities. It had no defence against riflemen who might shoot down from the rocks or even against a cavalry charge across the flat ground of the little valley. It did not take an experienced general to figure that out. Any ordinary trooper could have seen the disadvantages of the place. To Cal it was obvious. Too obvious.

He wondered what the renegade soldiers had been thinking about. The gun deal had fallen through and the girl had made her escape with the money. It must seem to them as likely, since their extended search had proved totally fruitless, that she had found her way back to her Mexican allies. So what would these renegades think of doing then? They still wanted the money, but an attack upon the Mexican camp would be a formidable undertaking, since they would know themselves to be outnumbered.

The only solution would seem to be that of leading the Mexicans into a trap. These would-be revolutionaries still needed the guns. They had come all this way and had already taken great risks to obtain them and would not be in a frame of mind to give up. There was no longer any possibility of renewed trust in the negotiations. Lives had been lost on both sides. There was little doubt in Cal's mind that the Mexicans themselves would be looking for a chance to attack, to take the guns by force, and to retrieve the money which they believed had been stolen from them.

So, it seemed to Cal, the trap had been set; the sleeping camp, with camp-fires big enough to burn for hours to light the Mexicans towards it, and the open ground, perfect for an attack by cavalry ... while all around, in the clefts of the rising rocks and in the thickets of gorse, would lie in wait the riflemen, well prepared for their deadly work.

But was he right in his suspicions? He whispered in the ear of Billy Crowfoot, who crouched beside him, the one word – 'ambush?' – and saw the dark head nod in reply.

'Look!' The Indian's finger stabbed towards the shape of boulders outlined against the fire-light. 'See soldier man?'

Cal stared as hard as he could but saw nothing until there was a faint movement, the hint of a pale face as it twisted around in the deep shadows. There was a man there, sure enough, lying in wait, stirring to ease his cramped muscles – or had he heard something from them: Cal's whisper or Billy's murmured reply? The soldier was a fair distance off but in the quiet of the night sound travelled. Cal himself thought he heard the faint, far-off sound of hoofs which died away at once. Perhaps a scout returning from spying out for the Mexican approach, or maybe even a Mexican rider making more noise than he should. It was impossible to guess. They lay perfectly still, hardly daring to breathe until they judged it safe to make a silent retreat.

As they climbed the slopes, Cal turned over in his mind the significance of what he had seen and tried to work out his own attitude towards it. There was going to be a battle and much loss of life but there seemed to be nothing that he could do about it. Since it was all merely gun-runners who were involved, maybe he should not be too concerned. They were all criminals. The guns were certainly stolen and the Mexicans had no right to be over the border on such a mission anyway. If they all shot one another up it might be a good thing for the law-abiding community. On the other hand, what he had seen of these renegades had disgusted him and this trap seemed a pretty low, shoot-in-the-back kind of set-up. Some of the Mexicans at least had patriotic motives for what they were doing, although that could not be said for them all. In that sense, they seemed a better bunch than this gang of renegade soldiers. Even so, he could not allow himself to put aside the memory of Heston and Puppy Grant being gunned down when the posse had suddenly come across the Mexican riders, although, even at that, he could understand the panic reaction of the Mexicans in that situation.

Nor could he forget the bullet that had almost finished him and the ball that had killed Juan Valdes. These things had to be settled and he was determined that they would be whenever the chance came, but what stuck in his mind and twisted like a knife was the look in the eyes of the man in the Reb cap as he stared at Maria. It was a look that had seemed to say: *I would sure like to keep ya for myself, honey, but I'm goin' to have to kill ya jest the same.*

So it was that Cal made up his mind to help the Mexicans, if he could, until such times as the renegade gun-runners had been settled once and for all.

The descent into the narrow, twisting tunnel

proved more difficult than the climb had been and Cal was even more acutely aware of his strained arm which pained him at every jolt and turn. As he descended, he made up his mind to take the risk of riding out of the gully in the hope of intercepting and warning the Mexicans who might well be already on the move. He would go himself and leave Billy and Maria safe in the cave until this fight was over.

The horses some way in from the cave mouth snorted in alarm as he felt his way past them. The second one shied away a little and he put out his hand to calm the third but found to his astonishment that there were only two animals there. Anxious seconds later and his fears were confirmed. Maria was nowhere to be seen. She had taken advantage of his absence to ride off without argument and alone....

There was no doubt that she was making for the Mexican camp to hand over the money she was carrying. That idea had been uppermost in her mind ever since their escape from the ambush. He had failed to convince her that there was danger from Salas or from any of the other Mexicans. It was possible also that she assumed that Salas and his immediate supporters were now dead and she had no need to fear Ibarra.

They led the remaining horses down the slope from the cave mouth and then set off at a canter along the gully in the direction from which they had come. It seemed obvious that she would ride that way since to go in the other direction would lead her into unknown territory and almost certainly she would be lost in the rugged landscape all around. This way she had some idea of how to find her way back, although there were great risks of riding again into trouble as she came near the spot where they had encountered the renegades.

They knew that the sound of the horses' hoofs upon the hard ground must be carried on the still night air to the soldiers waiting in ambush but there was no help for that if they were to have any chance of catching up with Maria. Probably it would be assumed that the sounds came from Mexican riders and safety catches on rifles would be loosened already as a result. They took some slight comfort in the idea. It meant that the troopers would not be likely to come out in search of them just yet.

The ride along the gully in the near darkness was not easy and only the sharp eyes of Billy Crowfoot were able to pick out that point where they had ridden down into it so many hours before. They pressed their horses into the slope and at length reached firm higher ground where grassy undulations of hillside spread out around them. There was no sign of Maria and it was possible that she had lost her way in the darkness but there was no help for it except to ride on, hoping for the best.

They crested a rise and then came to a sudden halt as they saw the horsemen almost upon them. There were five or six, almost in line abreast, carrying rifles at the ready across their saddle bows. Both parties gasped in surprise and Cal heard exclamations of alarm in Spanish. A gun was raised and aimed at him and as abruptly lowered. Then the rider to the front rode in closer, peering through the dim light. There came a subdued laugh and a sudden gleam of white teeth.

'Señor Rogers? I thought so. Lucky for you about white – eh – white cloth on your head, heh? Or you be dead with bullet already. Then maybe Injuns eat you up finally, heh?'

It was the muleteer who had first taken Cal into captivity, now riding a sturdy pony and ready to fight like any cavalryman. The others seemed of the same kind. Ibarra was bringing up all his men for this showdown.

'Sure, sure, maybe they will yet.' Cal felt that he should acknowledge the joke, although he was in no humorous frame of mind. 'But, listen carefully, have you seen the girl – the *señorita* – anywhere? She is going into danger. We must find her!'

'No, no seen the *señorita*.'

Cal's heart sank. He was becoming more and more convinced that Maria had lost her way altogether and would ride into trouble before he could protect her.

'Señor Ibarra? I need to speak to him. It is important.'

'Señor Ibarra?' There was a hint of doubt in the man's voice now as if he was suspicious of Cal's intentions. 'All right. I bring you to Señor Ibarra but I take your gun first, OK?'

They found Ibarra about half a mile further to the west. He was riding with a large body of men, lined up in charging formation, but moving at a slow speed. He had already learned from his scouts about the gringo camp about a mile ahead in which everyone seemed to be asleep. He had also been told that numerous beer bottles were scattered around the camp-fires and that there were men sleeping with their feet almost touching the hot ashes. He had assumed from this that all the dirty gringos had been drinking and were now oblivious to everything around them. The idea fitted in well with his general opinion of such men and it seemed to him that a well organized charge through the camp could bring the entire affair to a satisfactory conclusion very quickly.

When he heard what Cal had to say, he held up a hand to halt his men, and then asked to hear the details of the planned ambush once again. After that he stared at Cal very hard.

'I thought you had been killed by these soldier bandits,' he said quietly, 'along with Miss Valdes and some of my men. Señor Salas told me that he believed you and she had probably been shot and the money stolen. What is the truth? Where is the *señorita*?'

So, the clever Salas had made his escape from the battle in the draw! The knowledge leapt into Cal's mind without any suggestion of surprise. Very likely, Salas and his closest men had made a bolt for it when they saw how things had turned against them and had gone back to Ibarra with the tale of the soldiers' treachery but with no hint of their own. Where was Salas now? Out there in the night, busy with his next scheme to lay hands on that fortune? And if he was successful, his hands must be laid upon Maria also! The thought scared Cal so that he looked at Ibarra with sudden appeal, even as the silver of that murderous pistol caught the starlight.

'I think she is searching for you to give you back all that money. Have you not seen her? We've got to find her!'

Far off somewhere in the darkness, they heard a woman scream once, high-pitched, terrified.

SEVEN

'It is of no use to ride off into the darkness with no idea of where you are going or what enemies are waiting for you,' said Ibarra, his hand out to grip the bridle of Cal's horse. 'The *señorita* may have fallen in with these coyotes – and it grieves my heart to think of it – but it may be that her horse fell and she screamed in fright, or she may be a little hurt only. It is of no help to her if you ride into the bullets of the enemy.'

Cal held still, his heart pounding, anger and dismay flooding through his mind. His impulse was to gallop in the general direction of the scream, although he had little idea of where it had come from, but he could understand well enough, as did Ibarra, that the attempt would probably end in disaster.

'Also, my young friend, you have just informed me that my men are about to be

103

outflanked. I believe that you tell the truth and so I must have my men outflank the enemy. It will not do to have you ride towards their accursed camp before we are quite prepared.'

Cal saw that this was the main consideration as far as Ibarra was concerned. The Mexicans still needed the guns and also they wanted revenge. Maria was less important to Ibarra, however high in his estimation was her beauty and courage.

'Maria has all the money with her,' put in Cal, his hot anger turning to a cold hatred. 'That must be interesting to you.'

'Yes, I believe she has.' Ibarra was staring back at him, fending off his anger with anger of his own. 'I am certain that she intends returning it to us. She is a lady of honour. I am aware of her goodness and courage but I am also a patriot and my duty comes first. You understand?'

'I understand, all right,' answered Cal. 'Jest remember, while you're about it, that you're talking to a Texan, and if I was as much a patriot as I should be, I'd be takin' a damned poor view of this invasion of my country by a bunch of Mexican foreigners! You understand?'

'I see you do not trust me, Señor Rogers.' Ibarra smiled evenly. 'Well, that is too bad. I see also that you have noticed this fine old pistol in my belt? It is very old – about 1760, I think. I have always been very interested in such things. Señor Valdes knew that and presented it to me. It was very kind of him. I believe he meant it as a gesture of friendship and trust. Ah, well, we can do all our talking later.' He turned and spoke rapidly in Spanish to the men nearest to Cal and Billy, who closed around them. 'Now, I must go into battle.'

He turned away, giving out commands to his followers. The large band of riders began to split into two groups and to spread away from one another. Cal stared after him. So he was claiming now that Valdes had given him the murder weapon! If that was true then what a twist around of the knife it had turned out to be! And what about Valdes? A present to cement a friendship; to encourage mutual trust? Weird ideas about Valdes had begun to jump around like jack-rabbits in the back of his mind almost since the start of all this ...

'*Vamos!* Go! We go!' The muleteers were pressing them forward at the heels of the main body of cavalry. They rode on at increasing pace, surrounded at close quarters by men who kept a strict watch upon them while not treating them exactly as prisoners.

Soon the better-mounted men drew well ahead and vanished altogether into the shadows of the rising land on either side of the valley. Then, within some minutes of riding, Cal became aware of groups of horses standing under the control of a few muleteers, and he realized that some of the Mexicans had dismounted to gain the heights above the hidden renegades if at all possible.

He and Billy were told to stop and to hold themselves in readiness for any soldiers who might force their way out in a bid to escape.

'I need a gun,' growled Cal, exasperated. 'What can I do without a gun?'

'Sure.' The Mexican nearby passed over the six-gun which had been taken from him earlier. 'Señor Ibarra say it OK ... but no shoot us, or else....'

He left the threat unfinished. Cal held the gun in readiness, relieved to find himself again armed. Billy Crowfoot, he knew, had nothing but a knife, but it could not be helped.

The shooting started within minutes. There came flashes through the far darkness and the thunderous fire of many rifles, accompanied by shouts and occasional screams of pain. It went on for some time, then a man in a blue tunic and armed with a rifle came running through the half-light. When he saw the group of Mexicans he turned in the other direction, letting off a wild shot as he did so. Cal fired back and saw the man stumble as the bullet took him in the leg. Then a Mexican spurred his pony forward and struck out with a long machete. The soldier fell without a sound, his neck sliced almost through.

A moment later three horsemen came galloping by. These also were troopers, wild-eyed and fearful. It was obvious that they had felt themselves to be in desperate danger and had reached their mounts to make an attempt to ride their way out of it. The mounted muleteers closed with them and a savage, close-range fight ensued. Soon, the troopers lay dead and a Mexican groaned under a smashed shoulder.

The shooting amid the boulders and scrubland around the camp went on for a long time. Many of the troopers were good marksmen and put up a determined resistance. The Mexican casualties became heavier and their mood became the more savage as a result. Soon the understanding spread that no prisoners were to be taken, and as the firing gradually ceased wounded men were finished off by sabre or knife until no trooper still on the field of battle remained alive.

In the near silence that followed, the Mexicans moved into the camp, some on horseback, a good many on foot. Cal found himself riding in with them and watched as the dummy sleepers of canvas, wrapped in blankets, some with boots sticking out, were turned over and kicked aside in derision.

He dismounted, keen to see the contents of the wagons and found that, of the three, two contained only cooking gear and food, while the third had a supply of guns; perhaps 300 mixed rifle-muskets and smoothbores, probably captured from the Confederates after the war and kept in some depot for years before they were stolen.

So these were the arms that had prompted this Mexican invasion and had been responsible for all the killing that had followed. Cal was not too surprised. It had seemed to him from his observations from the hill that there were only three wagons in the camp and a few mules nearby – nowhere near enough to transport the huge haul of arms that the Mexicans had come prepared for.

How was it possible that Juan Valdes had been fooled in this way? Had he not seen in advance what was to be given to the Mexicans in return for that large amount of money? Or were these arms just a blind to be shown around the camp at times in case any Mexican scouts might be observing from afar? Even so, it could not have fooled Juan Valdes, who had been given the task of negotiating the deal.

'Holy mother of God!' Ibarra was raging in his chagrin. 'Is there no honour to be found amongst these vermin? Can this be all there is? No, no, surely not! We must search as soon as the light comes. There must be more wagons and more guns!' He strode about the camp, yelling out more orders in Spanish, while his men bowed their heads before the storm of his rage.

There were not so many Mexicans around now. Cal noticed the fact and realized that the renegades had sold their lives dearly. Those men still alive were occupied in carrying in the dead and wounded and their expressions had dropped from elated triumph to something close to despair.

His own mind was clouded with despair also. All through the night of battle he had heard over and over again in the depths of his soul that scream which had echoed through the darkness and which he knew had been that of Maria. Now he stepped away from the wagon and walked to the edge of the camp away from the fading firelight. The sky told him that daybreak would come within an hour and then he might have a chance of finding her. The notion of finding her brought as much terror into his heart as hope. In fact, it seemed to him that she must be badly hurt or dead since she had not been seen or heard after that agonized cry of fear or pain.

He became aware of Billy Crowfoot standing beside him and he knew that the Indian's thoughts were much the same as his own.

'We try to find Miss Valdes when day come,' said Billy quietly. He was carrying a loaded rifle which he had picked up from the battlefield. He examined its straight length of barrel thoughtfully. His mouth tightened grimly. 'Maybe we kill somebody.'

'Yes, perhaps we shall find the brave *señorita*. Certainly we shall try. I hope she still lives.'

The voice came from behind them and Cal half-turned to see Salas standing there, reloading his revolver. The Mexican had a sneer lingering at the corner of his mouth and Cal felt a strong temptation to strike out at him. He had not seen Salas since the ambush in the gully and now to see him and hear him in this situation was hard to bear.

'It'll be no thanks to you if she is still alive,'

snapped Cal, 'and God help you if she is dead.'

'You are becoming hostile, I see, Rogers, and perhaps a little foolish. Remember that Señorita Valdes took up the task of her late father of her own free will. She knew of the danger but her sense of honour gave her the courage to face it. We shall find her, never fear.'

'And the money?'

'And the money, of course. Would you have it any other way?'

Cal walked away from him, feeling the need to restrain his anger at this time. He could do nothing about Salas just now. If he turned on the Mexican leader he would be brought down at once by half a dozen bullets from his followers. His death would be of no use to Maria. Only by curbing his temper could he hope to help her. After that, it might be possible to settle matters with Salas.

Light broke suddenly over the peaks to the east as Cal and Billy Crowfoot mounted and rode back up the little valley. Their notion as to where they had heard Maria's cry was vague but they set off in a south-westerly direction and kept their eyes open and their senses alert every yard of the way.

Their search was at first quite fruitless. All

111

around were the tracks of scores of horses in the dust and pebbles. There was no way of picking out any that might have been made by Maria's horse. To their relief they did not come across any sign that she had come to harm either, though they spread the search wider and wider in the hours after sun-up.

At last, Cal called a halt to try to think things out. 'Billy, you know the country hereabouts better than most. If you was on the run from the Mexicans which way would ya go?'

Billy jerked his head slightly to signify back across the valley.

'Me, I would go thataway. Then take over hills. Low hills. Easy riding, after git outa this rocky stretch. After hills, some more rough country for good hiding-places. I think maybe I could lie low there until the Mexes go back home. That's if I had grub. Water I could find there 'cause I know places.'

Without another word Cal turned his horse and led off in that direction. Billy rode alongside and then gradually stole a little ahead so that he could use his tracker's eyes. The valley was left behind and they began to climb through more rough and barren country which held beyond it the promise of easier riding. But Billy shook his head as they went.

'Maybe this kind of crazy. I guess you think that Miss Valdes been taken off by some of them soldier bastards. That right? OK, so maybe I git on their trail. Then when we catch up what do we do? There could be six or seven or who knows how many of them, so what do we do with one rifle and a six-gun and a bad arm, heh?'

Cal had thought of it too. There might not be much chance. It would depend on how many there were and if they had taken Maria as a hostage then she would be the first to suffer. The idea of her being a hostage made him cringe but the other thought – the other possible reason for these scum making her a prisoner almost made him sick. All through the search he had half-expected to find her lying dead, but every hour in which there was no sign of her filled him further with horror and dismay as he thought what might happen when these rats came to believe that they had put plenty of miles between themselves and possible pursuit, and could find a little time to rest and amuse themselves.

For that reason, above all others, he felt the need to push on. He guessed that Billy thought it wiser to go back for some help from the Mexicans who would not fail to give them support when they knew the money was at stake. But Cal could not do that. Maria was being taken away from him and was in grave danger. He must try to find her without more delay.

Somewhere about mid-morning at a place where the grass was beginning to show again through the rock dust they came across some Indians, making a little fire to cook a snake. They looked at them with a mixture of curiosity and wariness. Billy spoke to them in native dialect and they waved scrawny arms over the nearest ridge, and then pointed to the ground. There was a little horse-dung there, still wet.

'They say there were four horses.' Billy Crowfoot was looking into Cal's eyes with an intensity that seemed to penetrate his mind. 'Three men with guns. One woman with arms tied up good. Injuns think they look like they gonna kill her. Sorry I to say that but that's what they say. But maybe not too many for us to fight, heh?'

They crossed the ridge to find the ground becoming softer and showing signs of tracks in the bending grass. Billy grinned and nodded his satisfaction. Cal felt his nerves go tense as he wondered uselessly which tracks had been made by Maria's horse. They pushed on as fast

114

as their tiring mounts would take them.

In the afternoon, however, they were forced to stop for rest. Their horses were approaching exhaustion and it would have been foolish to push them further. Billy found a place where there was a trickle of spring-water emerging from the hillside. They and their animals drank gratefully as they rested, although Cal found that he could not relax even for one moment.

After about an hour, they mounted up and climbed to the next rise of hill. There the country spread out below, green and welcoming. There was no sign of the troopers or their captive. Billy Crowfoot scanned the landscape ahead and then turned to look back the way they had come. He gave a grunt of surprise.

'Mexes,' he said. 'They catch up quick.' In the distance, just crossing the crest of a hill, could be seen a party of Mexicans. Cal counted eight. They were still too far away for their features to be distinguished but Salas's horse was there, white flanks gleaming in the sun.

EIGHT

They waited where they were until the Mexicans came up with them. There was no sense in doing anything else. Cal's distrust of Salas lay in the front of his mind but now that they were so close there was no way of avoiding this meeting.

'Ah, Señor Rogers, you have been leading us a dance, I see.' Salas smiled in seeming good humour, his eyes still cold and hard. 'One of my men saw you cross the little valley, otherwise we might have been too late to come to your assistance. Good fortune and then a band of Indians helped us on our way. I take it that you have not yet rescued the beautiful *señorita*?'

'No,' answered Cal bitterly, then with some irony, 'and we haven't rescued the money either.'

'Of course, the money. Is it not strange that

117

the conversation turns inevitably to the subject? Perhaps it is of as much interest to you as anything else?'

'Not to me, Salas.' Cal dropped all pretence of politeness. 'I only want to find Maria, that's all. I know that the money is the only reason that you're here.'

'Not quite, Rogers. The money, when we retrieve it, will go back to its proper purpose.' He glanced swiftly at his men, and then back to Cal. 'It will be used to buy more arms for our glorious campaign of freedom.'

Cal found himself looking at Salas's followers also. Two were heavily bearded and he felt almost certain that he had seen them with the so-called bodyguard that Salas had commanded at the time of the ambush. One of these stared at him now in a manner that reminded him of the man who had stared so fixedly at his wagon in the stillness of the night. The others were younger men whom he could not remember having seen before.

'I too wish to save the lady,' went on Salas, 'so we have good reasons for catching these bandits. It is as well that we came up with you on time or you might have – what do you say? – bitten off more than you can chew! What an ugly language is English.'

'Ugly as hell,' grunted Cal, losing all patience, 'but we generally mean what we say.'

Billy Crowfoot had been watching them both keenly throughout the short conversation but now he drew ahead a little to study the ground.

'Your Indian tracker is good?' asked Salas.

'Sharp as a razor..'

Billy led throughout the long day, rarely losing sight of the trail even for a few minutes. From time to time he seemed at fault where the surface rock thrust through the thin hill grass but always he picked up the trail. Once, Cal saw the Indian's neck stiffen and looked past his shoulder to the horizon but saw nothing but uneven peaks and crests amid the shallow sea of rough sun-toughened vegetation. Within a second, Billy's eyes were again on the ground but as they passed, some time later, a rocky outcrop, the Indian glanced in its direction as if it might have held some significance for him.

At length the tracks began to lead off to the west in a ragged, doubtful line, as if the riders ahead were unsure of where they were going. The hills gave gradual way to more rock and drifting sand and rugged contours. Then Billy spoke for the first time in hours.

'They know we on their trail,' he said shortly. 'Best keep look-out.'

The Mexicans sat up straighter in the saddle and drew their rifles from their gun boots. There had been little conversation amongst them all day. The younger men spoke softly in Spanish to one another once in a while but Cal noticed that the two older, bearded men said nothing at all, and Salas's loquaciousness had come to an abrupt end. It seemed to Cal that there was an air of tension amongst the Mexicans, almost as tight as that which existed between Salas and himself.

Some time in the late afternoon, they came by an abandoned shack with a caved-in roof and one wall flattened to the ground. There was an old barrow nearby and a heap of rubble. Off to one side a huge hole in the earth showed where old-time miners had been at work when gold had been found in the region. Salas looked around suspiciously but there was nothing of note to be seen and Billy led on without hesitation.

The area had been heavily mined for a couple of years in the distant past and there were signs of more excavations at almost every twist and turn. The Mexicans grew increasingly nervous as outcrops of rock towered above them, suggesting the possibility of ambush. Billy's remark that the troopers knew they were being followed held the threat of just such a trick and the riders glanced warily on all sides as they went.

The ground beneath them was coarse sand mixed with pebbles, and the tracks of the soldiers' horses could be plainly seen, even by less experienced eyes. Although the shifting surface gave no clear outline of horseshoes, the lines of disturbed surface material gave ample sign of their passage. Following this trail, they rounded a slope of scree and mining rubble and saw, some yards up, the square entrance to a mine, kept open partly with the help of crumbling pit-props. At the sight, Salas drew in his breath sharply and raised his revolver. His followers drew the safety catches of their rifles. All thought that it was a place where an ambush might be attempted, but Billy Crowfoot held up a reassuring hand.

'Is OK,' he said, grinning. 'Tracks go on past. See?'

He was right. The trail continued undisturbed along the narrow track and round the next bluff. In minutes they had left the empty threat behind them.

'They go pretty slow,' observed Billy. 'They tired. Need to rest soon.'

They rode on, expecting at almost any

121

moment to find themselves faced at last with their armed and desperate quarry. Cal was racked with inner doubts at the prospect. Even if he and the Mexicans could outshoot these men, what chance would Maria have? It seemed obvious to him that she would die in the conflict, probably as the result of a mean and spiteful bullet as the troopers felt themselves to be on the verge of defeat. Just the same, it seemed that there was no other course open to him except to go into the attack in the wild hope of saving her.

Billy continued to lead the way over the rocky landscape. Only when the light failed did he draw his mount to a halt.

'No good go on any more,' he said. 'Too dark now.'

They settled down to spend the night where they were. There was no suggestion of making a fire for fear that it would be seen by the troopers who might then think of making a surprise night attack. One of the younger men was detailed to keep watch and took up his position near to the horses. There was a suspicion in the air as to the intentions of Cal and Billy so they were deprived of any chance of riding away in the night.

Cal lay as far as he could from the Mexicans,

all of whom lay back in the dry grass and covered themselves with blankets, grateful enough for the opportunity of some rest. There was deep breathing all around when he heard Billy whisper in his ear that they should both slip silently away into the grass and down the nearest slope.

They crept like snakes for what seemed a long way before the Indian rose cautiously to a stooping position and went into a half-run. Cal followed and then straightened up so as to make better progress when they felt it was safe to do so. It seemed to Cal that he was being led back in the direction in which they had recently come.

'What's the idea?' he grunted hoarsely, fighting for breath.

'You not trust Salas, eh? Me neither,' answered Billy, without slackening his pace in the slightest. 'He all set to finish us off when he reckon good time come. We git Miss Maria ourselves. Then git to hell, pronto.'

'Maria? How come? You know where she is?'

'Sure. In old mine with soldiers.'

'But the tracks ... You said—'

'Sure. Tracks go right past mine then away round over hard stone. These buzzards ride right around bluff and then back in mine. Then sweep tracks away. Like me at cave. Only they sweep too hard. Turn up dark dirt to top instead of dry sand. Then they leave bit of wood up near mine door. It all scraped and shiny on one side after their fool sweeping.' He chuckled under his breath. 'Stupid fellers, heh?'

Cal could just about see it in his mind; the troopers, realizing that they were being over-taken, but unable to make better speed on near-exhausted horses. Then the decision to hole up in the mine, hoping to be bypassed but prepared, of necessary, to engage in a gun duel from that defensive position. It was much preferable to being caught in the open by a superior force. Their preparations had not been quite good enough, though, to fool Billy Crowfoot.

'We're just about there, ain't we?' Cal asked after they had run about a mile over the rough ground and the top of the bluff was in plain view against the night sky.

'Jest about. Say, Mr Cal, time to take that goddamned thing off your head. It's jumping around in the dark like a jack-rabbit tail.'

Cal tore the bandage off, wincing slightly as the dressing ripped away from the wound. As he did so, he caught a glimpse of movement on top of the bluff and threw himself down. A man was there, standing very still, and looking all around over the darkened landscape, with his head slightly on one side as if listening.

They lay in mute silence, like wild animals, uncertain whether they were the hunters or the hunted. At last, after many minutes of careful watching, the man turned away and vanished.

'They leave now,' hissed Billy. 'Now we need to move in.'

They climbed up the slope as quickly as they could in their weariness, crossed the stony ridge which ran down that side of the bluff, and scrambled down the other side amongst the boulders. From where they now were they could see the steep slide of scree which had formed below the mine in decades past, but they were out of sight of the entrance. To move out further to get a view of the entrance would have meant drawing away from the defence offered by the rocks. They lay in wait, guns ready but with no plan discussed between them. Both assumed that the only thing to do was to shoot down the troopers before they had time to harm Maria – if she was still alive. The thought that she might already be dead or harmed burned like a hot coal in Cal's mind and he vowed to kill them – kill them all – if that was so....

The starlight shed just enough light to make

shooting with accuracy a possibility. The range was short enough for a six-gun and easy for a rifle. They did not have long to wait. There came the sound of a hoof from the vicinity of the mine and then further clatter as a horseman emerged. He came into sight, reining in his mount hard to keep control as it descended the unsafe gradient to the trail beneath. He was a tall man wearing a broad hat with a hint of white kerchief at his neck. When he reached the trail he hesitated for a second to look around and then, to Cal's relief, turned his steed to pass near the spot where they crouched in readiness. The second rider came close behind the first and was followed immediately by the dim outline of Maria, mounted on a grey, and leaning forward as if in pain and distress. From where he was, Cal could not tell whether she was injured or ill and exhausted but the sight of her weakened form drove him into a fury which he could hardly control. The last rider, bare-headed but clad in a buckskin jacket, held a hand-gun which he seemed ready to use on her if there was any attempt at escape.

In the semi-dark, Cal's features tensed in hatred. His six-gun, already raised, quivered in his deep anger. Finger tightening on the trigger, he took swift aim, knowing that this man with

Maria's life in his hands, must be killed first of all, before the vengeful and spiteful bullet could be loosed upon her.

As Cal pulled the trigger, Billy's rifle boomed out from nearby and the man leapt in the saddle with a gurgling scream. It looked as if he had taken both bullets, one in the face and the other somewhere in the body. His gun flew from his hand and he toppled to the ground while his horse reared in fright.

At once, Cal swung his arm to bring down the next man. There was no time to be spared. In a second the remaining troopers would recover from the surprise and would retaliate with Maria still out there in the gravest danger. His bullet took the man just in front of Maria in the lower body and he doubled up in the saddle while his rifle dropped to the ground. He clung on desperately as his agitated horse spun around, blocking Cal's view of the trooper to the front.

At that, Cal found himself running down the rough slope and across the trail towards Maria. His mind seemed suddenly to be in a wild panic out of fear for her safety. When he reached her, he grabbed at the reins of her horse and then discovered to his immense consternation that her hands were tied to the saddle-pommel.

Mouth set in a tight line, he slashed at the cords with his knife, felt them snap, and then caught Maria as she fell towards the ground.

A bullet sang past his head. Then came the sound of many hoofs. He looked up to see the surging shadowy mass of riders cantering down the trail. There came shouts in Spanish and he caught sight of Salas's white horse in the throng. Another bullet ripped into the trail at his feet. He pulled Maria up and carried her in a stumbling run to the cover of a boulder nearer the mine entrance.

The trooper who had been at the head of the little cavalcade had already spurred his horse onward when the first shots were fired but now he pulled up in fright and indecision. The mob of horsemen was almost upon him but he recovered himself sufficiently to fire into them. For all his terror, his ability as a marksman did not desert him. He brought down two Mexicans before a hail of bullets destroyed him and his horse in a bloody, heaving mass that momentarily almost blocked that narrow part of the trail.

Cal lifted Maria again. This time she found her feet and they staggered together up to the mine mouth, where she slumped to the floor. He turned swiftly, gun again in hand, and saw Billy

Crowfoot loose off another shot at the horse-men. A man yelled and jumped from the saddle. The others were already dismounting and making for the nearest cover as Billy turned and ran along the short length of trail and up towards the mine. As he went, he stooped suddenly to pick something up. A lone horse-man appeared behind him, rifle raised. In that second, Cal recognized Salas and knew at once what Billy had found. He fired without hesita-tion and saw the Mexican reel in the saddle and then back off with all speed.

'Got him straight in the shoulder,' growled Cal to himself with grim satisfaction.

Billy Crowfoot did not slow down for an instant in his run for the mine entrance. He reached it, all out of breath, and dropped some-thing to the ground. Cal recognized it as the bag of money which Maria had carried with her earlier and which he had just seen hanging from the saddle of the second trooper.

'God, do we need that?' he yelled. He was disgusted by the sight of it. It seemed to him to have been the cause of all their troubles.

'Jeeze....' Billy grinned and shrugged help-lessly. 'Sorry. Just seemed too much to leave lying around.'

NINE

'You hurt, Maria?' Cal asked the question,
almost without looking at her, his eyes still
questing the dark outlines of rock and scrub for
any sign of a renewed attack.

'No, Cal … Oh, God, Cal. How did you get
here? Thank God! Oh, thank God!'

'Are ya harmed, Maria, in any way?' he asked
insistently, dreading the possible answer.

'No, no, they just pushed me around. They
caught me in the dark when I was trying to
get back to Ibarra. Maybe I shouldn't have left
you, Cal. No, of course, I shouldn't have! I
must have been mad or stupid but I knew you
would never agree to it because of the way you
distrusted him.' She sounded almost hysteri-
cal and he put out his hand in the dark to grip
her arm comfortingly. 'But they just wanted
me as some kind of a hostage, while they stole

the money, at least that's what …'

Yeah, that's what you think, he commented inwardly, but things would have changed later when they had made a good getaway. Aloud, he said, 'It's great to see ya safe, Maria,' and then thought how stupid a remark that was with all these Mexican polecats waiting to gun them down.

There was a long, long silence. Then came the roar of a rifle and a bullet struck into the roof of the mine just inside the entrance, sending a shower of dirt down upon them.

'Rogers!' It was the voice of Salas, not too far off, probably in the rocks almost opposite the mine. Cal did not answer. He was listening carefully for any suggestion of footfalls, seeing, in his imagination, men creeping in to attack under cover of this attempt at parley. He was also listening for something else that he felt he had detected in the Mexican's voice.

'Rogers! So you are a thief! You steal the money of our patriots!'

Yes, it was there … that trembling note of pain that spoke of a severe wound. Salas had been hit hard.

'Rogers, we will kill you. We shall stay and shoot and shoot until you are all dead! You have no escape. You will die – and the *señorita* also –

and that Indian half-mule!' Salas sounded mad
with fury and frustration and fierce pain. 'You
are trapped. We can kill you all and then have
our money. It is a matter of a little time only!'

That was true. It was just a matter of time. If
the Mexicans kept up this siege then they must
win. Cal knew that they had food and water
with them and firepower enough to foil any
attempt at a breakout. There was no food or
water in the mine and, for that matter, not very
much ammunition. Also, in spite of the Mexican
casualties, the odds were still in their favour.

But they had a weakness. It was in the voice
of Salas. It told of an agony growing worse with
every minute that passed. It seemed likely that
his shoulder had been smashed and must be
crying out for medical attention. A prolonged
siege could only be one long torture for Salas
and death could step out into his path before
the end of it.

Nevertheless, there was the question of the
money – that fortune in US dollars which lay in
the bag at Cal's feet. That meant almost everything to Salas. Of that, Cal had no doubts. The
Mexican would step to the edge of his own grave
to have it for himself.

'Rogers, for the sake of the Revolution, I am
prepared to make a deal.'

The Revolution? Why did he keep on with that pretence? Salas had long intended the money for himself. That had been clear to Cal since he had seen the soldier in the Reb cap having his brains blown out by the Mexican bullet and had felt the next one almost doing the same for himself. But, of course, the pretence still existed for the young Mexicans who still stood in support of Salas. They seemed sincere in their ideals. It was often the way....

'Rogers, are you hearing me?'

'Sure, I'm listening.'

'Return the money to us and we will ride away from here and leave you safe! That, I promise.'

'It is not his ...' Maria was sitting up, her face pale and anxious looking in the dim light. 'It must go to Ibarra. Salas cannot be trusted. You know that, Cal.'

Cal stared at her dim outline. There never was a more idealistic girl than Maria, he thought, nor one so slow to believe the worst of anybody. But she was wrong in this. There was no possibility of giving the money to Ibarra. Salas would have it or die in the attempt. Even if he died first, then his men would press in the attack and kill them all, as promised, and still take the money.

134

He leaned over and spoke into her ear, softly, so that his words could not float out on the still night air. 'Maria, we've been up to our necks in this long enough. We can make a deal with the money. If we don't, then we're dead. That's for sure.' The earnestness of his tone impressed her and she fell silent.

'So,' he continued, 'I'm not goin' to let you get killed – not if I can help it.'

He shifted forward slightly so that his voice might carry the more easily but kept his head just behind the heavy wooden prop which held up the roof.

'Salas! All right. We can make a deal. The money's yours but we need three horses brought up here into this mine. You got that? Send them up with one of your men and he'll come to no harm.'

There was silence. Cal imagined Salas struggling out there in the dark to control his pain, to prevent it distorting his voice so much as to suggest weakness.

'Very well, Rogers.' The reply came at last with forced strength, faltering, nevertheless, over the words. 'You may have your horses. Do we ... do we have your word. No shooting? There must be no foolish ... shooting. Tell ... your Indian. Make sure, or you die ... and there ... it will end.'

'You have my word on it! Make sure the man is not armed.'

Once again, there was a prolonged silence, then came the sound of movement, footsteps and the tramp of a horse being led around, accompanied by half-whispered, urgent instructions in Spanish. A shape appeared on the trail which soon resolved itself into a Mexican leading a horse. He hesitated for a moment at the foot of the slope and then, at a signal from Cal, led the animal up and into the shaft. He was one of the younger Mexicans, lean and handsome, and the starlight caught his expression of contempt as he glanced at the Texan thieves who had attempted to steal the money of the revolution.

'Leave it there,' said Cal evenly, 'and bring the others. One at a time.'

The instructions were carried out and soon three horses, one being Maria's own horse, were tethered a yard or so in from the entrance. The young man stood looking at Cal with an air of expectancy tempered by a suggestion of indifference. Cal pointed to the bag of money.

'Take it. Then move out sharp.'

The Mexican dropped to one knee and opened the bag. From it he lifted out thick wads of notes and held them up in turn to the available

136

light. It was the first time Cal had seen anything of the contents of the bag. It obviously contained many thousands of dollars.

'It's all there,' said Maria, sounding wearied and dismayed.

The young Mexican nodded, thrust the bundles back, and rose to his feet. On his way down the slope, he turned abruptly and spat on to the ground.

They scarcely moved for the rest of the night. Cal and Billy took turns to keep watch and slept fitfully in-between times. The Texan dawn came up in its sudden burst of splendour, spreading golden light over a sour landscape. There was no sign of life outside except for a few vultures high overhead. On the trail sprawled the corpses of the three troopers, each in its own twisted portrayal of death, and the carcass of a horse, legs outstretched. Beyond this shambles could be seen the silent forms of two Mexicans laid out straight on the ground, sombreros placed, with some attempt at reverence, upon their faces.

They scrutinized their surroundings for a long time, suspicion deep in their minds, but saw nothing move and heard no sound. Then Billy crept outside and up to the top of the bluff to have a good look around, but came back to report that all was quiet. Only then did they set out, taking the trail back over the way they had come.

They had not gone far when Billy pointed out the track which told them that their enemies had taken the same route hours before. At that, Cal wondered whether to attempt to find their way back by some other way, but Billy Crowfoot said that it might be a mistake as the chances of becoming lost in the barren land were considerable. The Mexicans, in any case, were well ahead, and seemingly in a hurry to get away. Cal nodded his head in quiet agreement. Salas needed to have that wound attended to as soon as possible. There seemed little doubt of that.

He was right. Salas was at that moment making good time towards safety – as he saw it – but Cal, for once, underestimated his hatred and his ruthlessness. Within a mile of the mine, when they were trotting over a flat stretch under a slope of scrub, two shots rang out and Billy yelped and swayed in the saddle. For a second it was as if he would fall but he held on, pointed up the hillside, and spurred his horse in that direction, drawing his rifle as he went.

There came the boom of another shot and then Billy's horse seemed to scamper to one side and a Mexican, in a red jacket, leaped like a

138

startled rabbit out of cover. Billy's rifle swung and fired and the man dropped. By now Cal was galloping up the slope just in time to see a second man turn his rifle upon the Indian. Cal fired with his six-gun, once, twice, and brought him down in a writhing heap amid the scrub.

They searched around, ranging back and forth across the slope, but found nobody else. Then they went back to look at the attackers. They were young, one being the man who had exchanged the horses for the money. A true Mexican patriot, thought Cal, encouraged no doubt by Salas to hold back and take the revenge which he could not carry out himself. A fine way too of being rid of those of his party still idealistic enough to believe that he had in mind a selfless use for that fortune in banknotes.

'Maria, you're not hurt, are ya?' He rode anxiously down the hillside, as he saw that she had dismounted.

'No, but my horse is. One of the bullets hit his leg. Oh, God! It's pretty well smashed.'

It was bad. The leg was broken and hanging limp and useless. There was nothing to be done but to destroy the animal. Cal shot it, his heart heavy at the necessity, while Maria turned away in tears.

'These Mexicans must have had horses with them,' reasoned Cal. 'Look around, will ya, Billy?'

'Just little minute,' Billy was stooping slightly in the saddle. Need coupla' minutes.'

'You hit?'

'Yeah, no too bad ...' He was tearing at the tail of his shirt and strapping a length of it around his chest, under cover of the remainder. 'Soon be OK ... maybe you see about ... horses.'

Cal looked at him keenly. He then rode up over the crest of the hill and found the two Mexican ponies ground-tethered. When he came back, Billy was sitting up straight, smiling. 'OK, now, jest little graze.'

He led them across the hill country throughout the forenoon. The sun was almost overhead when he pointed out something in the grass. It was another Mexican, young and with one arm done up in a makeshift sling. There was a bullet hole in his back.

They found Salas about an hour later. As Cal had guessed, he had a bad wound in the shoulder with bone protruding through the flesh. Also his neck was half-severed from a machete blow from behind. There was no sign of his tough, bearded companions or of the money.

'So much for the revolution,' said Cal, without looking at Maria.

Towards sundown Billy began to point out landmarks to them, a tall hill, a razor-back ridge, a far-off peak.

'Not too much riding, now,' he said. 'Soon find way easy.'

'How are ya feeling?' asked Cal. 'That wound hurting bad?'

'No bad,' replied Billy, 'only little wound. Be OK.'

The sun had almost plunged behind the darkening mountains. They were all wearied to the point of dropping from the saddle and had not eaten all day. Once they had stopped at a little waterhole Billy had found for them and had gratefully slaked their thirst. Only that had kept them going. Now they knew that they must stop to rest in the cool night.

'Here,' suggested Cal. 'This is as good a place as we're goin' to find.'

There were a few stunted trees, just enough to act as a windbreak as the rising mountain airs drew in the breezes from the surrounding land. Then the coolness would turn to cold.

'What's that?' cried Maria suddenly, pointing towards the skyline.

There was something moving there; a figure

141

against the dying light. It seemed to become aware of their presence at the same time as Maria spoke and halted to peer through the twilight. Then it began to approach with a queer ambling gait.

'What is it?' asked Maria in some alarm. 'A bear?'

'No bear,' answered Billy. 'Seem like Injun.' He sniffed audibly. 'Smell like Injun.'

He was right. The shape turned by slow degrees into that of an Indian, old, bent, grey-haired. He wore a black hat and supported himself on a stick. Cal looked at him closely through the shadows and then smiled grimly. He had felt the weight of that stick a few times, and its point.

'Hey, you, white man. You got whiskey?'

'No whiskey,' said Cal.

'You got food for poor Injun?'

'No food.'

'Me give you good trade for food. Better for whiskey. Me give gun for whiskey.'

'Gun? What do you mean?'

'This gun. Very good gun.'

He held something up against the faint red light of the dying sun. It was a gun, sure enough, a pistol, long-barrelled with a fancy handle and a glint of silver. Even in that poor

142

light, Cal recognized it as the old Spanish pistol.

'Let's have that gun here,' said Cal, stretching out a hand.

'You got whiskey?'

Billy Crowfoot shifted a little in the saddle and then withdrew his rifle. He held it across his knee without threatening the Indian directly. Then he spoke in the native dialect. After some hesitation, the Indian replied and then made a shuffling movement as if anxious to go. Billy raised his rifle slightly and looked sideways at Cal.

'He say he found it on body of a man 'way over there, some place.' He motioned vaguely with the point of his rifle into the shadows. 'Says the man was big with hair on his face. He thinks he was killed by a man on a white horse and two other men with hairy faces about two days past. Sounds like Mexes from what he says they looked like.'

Cal was silent. He was aware of Maria stiffening alongside him. 'Let's have the gun,' said Cal again.

'Whiskey,' insisted the Indian. Billy spoke once more and the Indian passed the pistol up to him.

'What did ya say?' asked Cal.

'I tell him that he steal gun from chief Mex. Ghost of big man come and shoot him when he sleeps.'

Cal held the gun in the semi-dark, feeling its weight and size. There was no doubt as to what it was. This was the gun that Ibarra had carried in his belt even though he had a modern revolver in his holster at his hip. It had seemed like a kind of trophy that he liked to show off almost as if he had picked it up on the field of battle. But he had claimed that he had been given it by Valdes.... Now, he was lying dead out there somewhere amongst the boulders, having been killed by his own comrades under the leadership of Salas. Well, Cal did not feel too much surprise at that. Salas would have had little chance of ever gaining the money which was supposed to finance the revolution so long as Ibarra was alive. So a chance had been taken to kill him just after the fight with the rene-gades on that morning when he had been searching around in the vain hope of finding more guns. After that, Salas had been told of the sighting of Maria and her two companions and had given chase.

'Let me see the gun.' Maria took it into her hands and felt it carefully all over, before hand-ing it back to him. For a long moment she said nothing, then she murmured, 'I am very tired.'

The little Indian had vanished like a ghost. It was almost as if he had never been, but for the pistol in Cal's hands.

TEN

They camped where they were without fire or food or drink. Weak exhaustion was spreading itself upon their minds like an invisible veil. Nevertheless, Cal thought it best to keep a watch and sat up for the first part of the night until he judged it time to wake Billy Crowfoot to take a turn. The Indian pushed himself up on his elbows from his blanket and nodded assent as Cal dropped back to fall asleep in an instant.

In the morning, they found Billy Crowfoot dead. When Cal pulled aside his blanket it was to see a mass of drying blood and a wound that Billy must have known to be fatal the moment he received it. They knelt and looked into his dead face for some time. His eyes were closed but his mouth still grimaced in pain although he had uttered no sound.

With difficulty, Cal lifted the body on to

Billy's horse and tied it securely under the bloodstained blanket. They then mounted up and went on their way, picking out the landmarks he had pointed out to them the day before.

They moved slowly, knowing the fatigue and thirst suffered by their animals, weighed down also by the thought of Billy's death. Maria had said no word since they had discovered his body and, in fact, very little from the night before. She looked ill with exhaustion and seemed to cling on to her seat in the saddle with great difficulty. Several times, Cal looked at her sharply and anxiously as she swayed a little but always she recovered herself quickly and rode on, staring straight ahead. About an hour after they had set off from the makeshift camp, when they were riding not far from the edge of a deep ravine, she spoke for the first time.

'I must stop for a minute or two, Cal.'

'Sure, we can rest here for a little while, but not long. We have to try to find water.'

'I know, but just for a few minutes.' She drew her mount to a halt and sat there in the saddle, looking at the ground and then into the sky as if troubled by some problem which defied solution. Then she dismounted and walked over to him. 'Let me see the Spanish pistol again, Cal.'

148

'Sure thing.' He undid the strap of his saddle-bag and pulled out the weapon, glancing at it with renewed interest as he did so. It was a fine-looking gun for its age with a shining barrel and ... but there was something that he had not seen in the dim light of the evening before; rust around the chamber and a narrow, almost hairline crack. Anyone who attempted to fire this gun, he suddenly realized, would injure or even kill himself, and the trigger hung slack and useless. This weapon had not been used in years – decades! It made an interesting trophy or it might have found a place in a museum, but as a weapon it was worse then useless.

'Jeeze.' His face registered his astonishment. 'This gun cain't fire! It was never used for-'

'Let me have it here.'

He passed it down to her, watching her face which had become impassive. She expressed no surprise and did not look closely at the pistol but carried it rapidly to the edge of the ravine and threw it in a glittering arc so that within a second it had vanished and he heard only the crash as it struck somewhere far below and scattered its fragments amid the unseen boul-ders.

'That was evidence, Maria,' he said quietly, knowing by her manner, by the tension which

149

he could see in her, that something in her mind hung by a thread.

She stopped with her hand on halter and looked up at him, eyes defiant. 'Evidence of what, Cal?'

'That Ibarra didn't have the gun that – that killed your father.'

'We don't know ...' The defiance went out of her and she seemed to shrink within herself for a brief moment. 'How do we know what guns he had? All right, so my father was killed by an old gun. Maybe Ibarra had something to do with it or maybe he didn't. We both saw Ibarra with an old pistol but does that mean it was that one? We don't even know for certain that Ibarra is dead. Whose word do you have for it? An old Indian? Maybe some other Mexican killed my father! We don't know who killed him. Perhaps we'll never know!' Her voice trailed off. Looking into her distressed eyes, Cal guessed suddenly that she did know, or that she suspected someone else, not Ibarra, but someone to whom a name could not be placed ... not yet, not just at this time. Her haunted eyes told him that, almost as if she said it out loud.

'Billy gave his life for me!' Her voice seemed to verge on hysteria. 'He wanted to bring me back safe because he cared for me and believed in my father....'

Cal dismounted and put his arm around her and then, when she was calmer, helped her into the saddle. He did not say anything for a long time but kept an eye on her as he rode on, leading Billy's loaded horse.

How many hours went by in this way, he did not know. He was aware only of the heat, his thirst, and the anxiety over her which consumed him. All around, the landscape seemed to be in a blur, a heat haze, that rose from the parched earth and hung on to his eyes and his mind like the all-enveloping web of some gross spider. The shapes of rocks and isolated boulders loomed up as if through mist, and he skirted around them with due care, with the instinctive caution of a horseman on rough ground. Then he saw two such boulders move and come towards him and a voice sang out: 'Well, if it ain't Cal Rogers! An' Miss Valdes! Hey, you're in a pretty bad way! Here, miss, let me help ya....'

He recognized young Tom Capaldi and, a little way behind him, Will James. They helped Maria to dismount and gave her water from a canteen, then Cal felt water being pressed to his own mouth also. He drank greedily and the mist began to clear from his eyes and mind.

'Gee, thanks, fellers,' he croaked, 'how did ya find...?'

'We've been scouting around all day, not lookin' fer you special, Cal. We reckoned you had been killed, to tell you the truth – but, well, the thing is, after that fight we had with the Mexes, Puppy Grant was killed an' the sheriff was real bad wounded an' Jem Marks had a broken shoulder an' we needed to git back fer help, specially when one of our boys comes in and says he seed a whole big bunch of Mexes, too many fer us to handle. Ryan reckoned we needed to call in the army, so he an' some of the others went back to Three Pines with Mr Heston an' Jem.'

'That's it,' put in Will James, 'but we and the rest stayed behind to keep a look-see and there's bin one helluva battle.... Say, but what about you and Miss Valdes?'

'We got kind of mixed up with the Mexicans,' said Cal in a level voice, 'but we managed to shake them off, you might say.' He did not glance at Maria. He knew that she was sitting nearby, staring into the ground. 'Only, Billy Crowfoot got killed. He was acting as guide to Miss Valdes. She, well, she was all upset about her father and came out, well, just to see if she could help, I guess.'

He did not really know what to say about it.

There was much that she wanted to remain unsaid. He felt pretty sure about that.

'Yeah, well, that was brave of her, but maybe you might have been better leaving it to the sheriff, Miss Valdes. This ain't no place for a lady.' Will sounded sympathetic and disapproving at the same time. 'But about that business, Cal. Ryan always reckoned he was looking for a Mex with an old gun – some kinda' old pistol – he told me and Abe, then yesterday we—'

'Yeah, we finds this little Mexican feller,' interrupted Tom, 'lying in the grass with a broken leg. He reckoned that after the battle with them soldiers—'

'Bunch of deserters!' growled Will.

'Yeah, like deserters or somethin', all of them killed though and near all the Mexes, by the look of it. Anyhow, the other Mexes have lit out south, back to the border. Anyhow, Will here, asks him—'

'About the pistol; damn me if a feller cain't tell his own story!' snorted Will. 'And he says that one of their leaders, a man called Ibarra, carried that kind of a gun. Did you ever see that feller, Cal, with an old pistol?'

'Sure, I guess I did, and the last time I saw him he had that kind of a gun.... He might be dead now, though.'

'Yeah? Well, that would just about wrap it all up and we could leave the army to sort out the rest, if they can. But, say, Cal, what about Billy?'

'Miss Valdes wants him buried back at her place.'

'Yeah, I understand. Sorry, we cain't escort you back. We got more scouting to do. You be all right? We kin give you food and more water and there's Snake Pit River a couple of miles ahead. OK fer the horses. You sure Miss Valdes be all right? She ain't looking so good.'

'I'll be fine, thanks, Will,' answered Maria speaking for the first time.

They parted soon after, Will and Tom moving off cautiously into the high country. There was no conversation between Cal and Maria for a long time, then she said: 'Thanks for not saying about the pistol, Cal.'

'What's the idea, Maria?'

'We'll leave it that Ibarra was seen with the Spanish pistol. It's all we know. It is enough.'

"Enough for the law, you mean?"

Again the silence; again the desperate unease in her eyes.

He shook his head sympathetically as he looked at her. How much did the law matter now? Best get her home....

It was a relief when they reached familiar country and he could have sung for joy when the Valdes land came into sight. He had imagined that it would be the same way for her but she seemed more tense with every yard of their approach and kept her face averted from him.

Field-hands waved when they saw her and one or two came forward, took off their hats and bowed their heads looking as if they wished to speak but somehow lacked the full courage. Then a foreman spoke to her in fluent Spanish. She listened gravely and uttered a word of thanks, as he led away Billy's horse with its silent burden. As they moved on, she rode a little ahead of Cal and he saw her back straighten and her shoulders set more squarely as if in sudden resolution. As they approached the house, he noticed that it seemed deserted but for a Negro burning straw and other rubbish in a small fire in the yard.

They dismounted and she went in without looking at him. He knew that there was something very wrong and stood in silent patience for some time. He looked around at the place with a new kind of interest, for the last few days had set his mind working in a way that it never had before. He had always known that Juan Valdes had problems about money but it was only now that his own eyes seemed open enough to see the signs of financial constraints in the buildings and the fencing and general upkeep of the farm. He guessed that there was much more that was unseen and had been unknown, probably, to everyone but Juan himself.

As he stood there waiting, the jack-rabbits of doubt that had plagued his mind regarding Juan Valdes again began to skip into his consciousness. He could understand, well enough, how desperate Valdes might have become for money to keep the place going and to provide for his family. The opportunity of making good money from helping the Mexican arms deal would have seemed too good to miss. Also, and this was the suspicion which Cal had found most difficult to accept at first, when Valdes became aware that the soldiers had no genuine deal to make, then the temptation to fall in with their plan to get the money without providing the guns might have been too great to resist – assuming he was being offered a handsome reward for his part in that piece of treachery. But he could only have agreed to that if part of the plan was to get rid of the Mexican leaders, otherwise there could be no future peace of mind for Valdes with the certainty of Mexican vengeance hanging over him and his family. For that reason,

Valdes had insisted that Ibarra and Salas should be at the final meeting – to be shot down before he took his share of the money. That was the way it had looked to Cal on the day of the ambush and it seemed no different now. Whether Valdes himself would have survived that meeting was very doubtful. Cal had seen in the eyes of the trooper with whom they had spoken an expression that allowed for no survivors and only the attempted double-cross by Salas had inadvertently brought about the survival of Maria and Cal and Billy Crowfoot on that day.

It was the only way that it all fitted together. Juan Valdes had allowed the threat of debt and perhaps poverty to turn him from a decent man into a thief and potential murderer.... Well, it had happened often enough before. What seemed unlikely, though, was that Maria would ever accept that, even if proof could ever be forthcoming. But there was no chance of that happening. What evidence there might have been was buried under the silence of the dead.

He waited there in the yard in silent dismay and then looked up as she came out of the house. He was struck by her calm dignity as she approached him. Her eyes, though, showed clear signs that she had been in tears just minutes before. In her arms she carried a small leather case and between her fingers there was what appeared to be a letter. She looked straight at him with the faintest of smiles and dropped the box into the flames of the little fire.

'You're right, Cal,' she said, seeing his look of surprise. 'It's a pistol case ... an old one, maybe a couple of hundred years old. My father had it for a long time. He was always interested in old firearms. It used to hold two pistols, a pair, in fact. One was useless but the other was still in pretty good condition. He must have given one of them to Ibarra as a gesture. I didn't know which one until you handed his to me. Then I knew that it was the good pistol which had been left in our house but had vanished on that terrible Sunday evening. That was what just about killed me, Cal, out there in the desert, more than the heat and the thirst. You see, my father sometimes loaded up that pistol and fired it off just in fun. Couple of times he even let Sebastian see him practise with it. I guess he left it lying around loaded that evening and Sebastian – well you know about him – he was never anything but a child in a growing body, and he could never tell the difference between playing a game and the real thing....'

'Jesus! You mean that Sebastian...?'

'Yes but I did not know. I could only guess.

When I got back from visiting Kate Martin that
Sunday evening, my mother said nothing, except
to repeat that my father had gone into
Baxterville. Now, I know that she had discovered his body not long before and had got rid of
the pistol. I did not think of it clearly until you
said something to me in the cave, then it all
began to fit together. I guess I didn't want to
think of it. It was too terrible. Next day,
Sebastian just sat grinning and eating his
breakfast. There was no sense in asking him
and I ... I was scared anyway of what his answer
might be. Deep down, I thought I knew the truth
and it seemed confirmed by the terrible, fearful
silence of my mother. She didn't rage against the
Mexican suspects. She said nothing – would not
even look at me – and could not bear to look at
Sebastian – so I think I knew, although I didn't
want to. So I thrust it aside. I thought only of
what I could do to finish what father had begun
– the noble work he had started....'

They were staring into one another's eyes.
'Noble work', thought Cal. Was there any point
in saying what was in his mind? The truth
about Juan Valdes was dead. It had been shot
down just when it was about to stand up in
plain view and what right did he himself have
to be judge and jury?

159

'Why do you tell me all this now, Maria?'

'This letter,' she dropped it into the flame with a little gesture of finality, 'was from my mother. She's gone. She has taken Sebastian with her and gone over the border. She won't be back ... ever.'

'Hell, but Sebastian wasn't really responsible. No jury would have convicted him of murder.'

'They would have taken him away, just the same; locked him up in one of these places for the criminally insane. My mother was always terrified of anything like that ever happening. She couldn't have stood that any more than he could.... To tell you the truth, I felt all the time I was away that I might come back to this.'

There was silence but for the faint hissing of the burning pistol case. For the first time it seemed that the place was quite deserted. Lives had been burned out in the flash of that ancient pistol and the conflagration that had followed. Maria's eyes were deeply troubled. It was as if something in her life had been savaged and she needed desperately to find healing. He smiled his understanding.

'Time to make a new start, Maria.'

She nodded and smiled back at him and placed her hand in his.

160